T

ABOVE THE TREES

A NOVELLA
by
Peter Larner

Books by Peter Larner

A Flaw in the Plan

Along the margin-sand

Covenant of Retribution

Covenant of Silence

Deathbed Betrayal

Deathbed Confessions

Farewell Bright Star

Harpoon Force

Lost in a Hurricane

One Christmas Past

Pawns

Sure Uncertainty

The Blue above the Trees

The Covenant Chronicles

The Old Explorers' Club

The Unfolding Path

Cover Design

Nina Patel

Dedicated to

Laura Molinari on her retirement from Hotel Belvedere, Bellagio. And with thanks to Tiziano, Giulia, Signora Lucia, and the Martinelli family for their incredible hospitality.

Isabella or The Pot of Basil
Stanza LIII by John Keats
(Based on a story from *The Decameron of Boccaccio*).

And she forgot the stars, the moon, and sun,
And she forgot the blue above the trees,
And she forgot the dells where waters run,
And she forgot the chilly autumn breeze;
She had no knowledge when the day was done.

THE BLUE
ABOVE THE TREES

1

St. Leonards, East Sussex

A rhythmic mélange of topics occupies the thoughts of JP Preparé as he climbs the stairs towards the study. Bedrooms, butterflies, Bellagio and the Hotel Belvedere. And now, the outline of a lecture is added to the list. He sighs heavily at the subject's lack of alliteration. His father would appreciate the word mélange, though why JP should care about such Francophile preferences is lost upon the world. Love, honour and reparation head the list of reasons. And strangely, one or all of them might be what Rhonda's decampment is about? He refused to call it an escape.

The study had been Lester's room when he was a teenager. His son gifted the larger second bedroom to his younger sister. Not through benevolence, as JP believed, but rather the indolent practicalities of keeping a smaller room tidy. Now the tiny space overlooking the oaks at the end of the garden is a mission control centre. It is a mission unconcerned with the butterflies and unperformed lectures that distracted the old man's contemplations. He senses a need to focus on the plan rather than an address that will never be delivered. Bedrooms, butterflies or undelivered lessons cannot provide clues to the whereabouts of his wife. They are merely notions bobbing on the foaming surface of lost time whilst any practical contact with recent events rests, undisturbed, submerged on a distant ocean bed. Auspicious clues are no more than reeds in the water, the refuge of life for the voice of the winds.

A fruitful plan develops like a butterfly, JP assures himself as he meanders around the upstairs rooms. Studying the curtains, he adjusts one side and snaps off a loose cotton thread. Everything needs to be tidy in preparation for Rhonda's return. But there was nothing to straighten or put away because nothing had been moved since he last tidied the bedrooms. Plans and butterflies, he pondered to himself. Such inconsequential allegories impress JP, especially when they are his own, and this was an exceptional one in his view.

Butterflies and plans have life cycles consisting of four stages of growth from conception to fruition. He nodded his head confidently, smiling at the originality of such a compelling analogical comparison. Perhaps he would suggest it to his former colleagues at East Sussex Sixth Form College. He might even use it himself if the Principal asked him to fill in for his young successor. He expected to be called upon during the Covid-19 pandemic, but the call never came.

Planning is metamorphic in its development. JP could hear himself addressing the class. A plan starts life as an idea that stirs in the chrysalis of the mind, rejects negative thoughts and takes flight, just like a butterfly. In a rare moment of whimsicality JP considered adding a humorous remark. "Copulation is not required," he mouthed, and the imaginary group of students laughed raucously. He immediately regretted the tailpiece and tutted loudly. What would The Principal think? Never mind that, what would Rhonda think? His wife gazes at him disappointedly from the windowsill.

He exits the room to escape her remonstrating stare and crosses the hallway to retrieve his journal. He needs to write these thoughts down. The comparison could be a precursor to a lesson on Henri Fayol's five functions of management.

"If planning is not the whole of management, then it is at least the greater part," JP declares to the framed picture of his wife. She returns fire with a scathing reply, stating the hurtfully obvious.

"You're retired."

He closes the window to protect her from a draughty wind that stirs the full-laden oaks at the end of the garden. The mellow hum of summer is switched off, and he looks at her again. He meant to do something with the photograph, but he can't remember what it was.

Each year JP planned the couple's annual holiday with military precision. His greatest enjoyment came from the success of the plan's execution. Rhonda's came from enjoying the product of his elaborate designs. In recent years they had all been customised, intricately organised by JP himself. Their last package holiday was eight years ago. This only replaced a customised vacation because it included visits to some inaccessible places. Well, unreachable without a car and JP never drove on holiday. Otherwise, it wouldn't be a holiday.

JP fingered one of the maps on the bed, unfolding it and smiling at his own ingenuity. No, he told himself, this isn't just another holiday. The plan this year isn't simply another plan. This is something completely different. This project requires a master plan that will develop past the larval stage of immaturity. The pupal stage would complete the metamorphosis, and a butterfly, in the shape of JP Preparé would take flight tomorrow on flight BA932 to Nice.

"Not Italy," he declared, picking up the photograph of his wife. She didn't seem as surprised as he had hoped. "Not Italy," he repeated as he sat her back down.

JP and Rhonda met at sixth form college, a coincidence possibly, or perhaps JP just felt an attachment to institutes of further education. Some people provide directions via pubs. Turn left at the Red Lion and then right at the Duke's Head. However, JP's life was directed by educational institutes. He and Rhonda hadn't met at the one he later worked in. They are all much of a muchness, Rhonda said, when he was rejected for a position a few years ago. The pair chose to go to the same university. By that time, he had been bitten, and she had been smitten, and they became inseparable. They were lost in each other's company, like a golf ball in the long grass, never to be discovered.

Once the butterfly analogy had been recorded, JP put down his journal and stood gazing into the second bedroom from the doorway. He could visualise the plan unfolding. However, in practice, this particular plan took the shape of several neatly folded piles of clothes. Ironed shirts, trousers with sharp creases, underwear, socks neatly balled into pairs and two ties just in case. The ties embodied the tiny degree of uncertainty in the plan. For JP could not be absolutely sure how the next few weeks might unravel. Despite his conviction to the contrary, it was unlikely his solo venture abroad would unfold as neatly as the shirts. And, although he wouldn't admit it, uncertainty unsettled him. It interfered with his yin and yang, confounding his temperament and competence in challenging situations or even less challenging ones. Change muted his ability to function normally. Unforeseen developments nudged him slightly out of kilter and unbalanced him. He would be seventy years old soon, and balance was becoming a problem, even when he hadn't been drinking.

He gazed in vagrant bewilderment at the shirts, sighing loudly. Those shirts were annoying him because he couldn't remember ironing them. Did it matter, he asked himself? Perhaps Rhonda ironed them before she left so abruptly.

"Without warning," he told himself. "No note explaining Rhonda's motives. No clue as to where she has gone. Just a packet of fish fingers and a stack of ironed shirts. She doesn't want to be found," he added, continuing to give himself support and advice.

It seemed a strange thing to do, though, iron your husband's shirts before leaving him. Which was another exasperatingly irritable issue. He couldn't remember exactly when it was she left him. It seemed like it was yesterday, but it must have been longer because the plan to find her had taken several days or possibly weeks to complete. He couldn't quite remember how long.

"It must have been several weeks since she left," he assured himself.

Forgetfulness or short-term memory loss was becoming a recurring problem, along with poor balance. He had lost the ability to put his underpants on without sitting down, and he could never remember putting his socks on whilst standing up.

"You're getting old," he groaned to himself.

"No, you're not," he could hear Rhonda reply in a faintly disapproving tone, for she detested self-pitying individuals. Blue Devils, she called them, though JP had no idea where the expression came from. It wasn't in the Oxford Concise English Dictionary, and he absolutely refused to look it up using Google.

Regular coastal walks and a morning exercise regime ensured that JP had the energy and physique of a younger man. Not a young man, but a markedly younger one than himself. And yet, he moved with slow intent, wandering patiently from room to room methodically, much as his mind worked. Everyone who knew him considered him a quiet, amiable man, serenely happy in his marriage and undeniably faithful. JP was loyal to his work, his country and, of course, to Rhonda. But, clearly, his wife did not share that loyalty because she had left him. He convinced himself that there wasn't another man, even though he knew there had been one in the past. But it was a long time ago, in the early days of their marriage. And, looking back, perhaps there had been more than one. She had confessed to one. He placed the palm of his hand across his mouth and admonished himself for such defamatory thoughts. What had Rhonda done to deserve such a malicious reckoning? An indiscretion of youth. Who among us is entirely innocent of such behaviour? Well, JP, for one. Not that the opportunity ever presented itself. Even in his youth, he was never the young lothario of the staff room.

A small notepad rested on the windowsill. The aide memoir was simply a list of tasks to complete before he slammed the door and jumped into the taxi. Watering plants, shutting the windows, emptying the fridge and switching off all the power points had all been ticked off. But something was missing. He suddenly remembered he needed to put the bins out before going on holiday. He smacked his forehead a little too firmly before gathering some rubbish from the bedrooms and proceeding downstairs to the kitchen.

JP spent most of his life steering clear of the neighbours, but today it couldn't be avoided. He went outside to the bins knowing his nosey neighbour would not miss the opportunity to infiltrate his well-guarded privacy. What was the difference between a nosey person and a caring one, JP thought to himself? JP's daughter was both, and his son was neither.

Someone had to know he was going away, JP assured himself. "Just in case," he added, although he hadn't really considered what eventuality he had in mind. JP admonished himself for a second malign smear on a member of his family. Well, a third if he included calling his daughter nosey.

"I'm glad I've caught you," came a familiar voice from across the low fence at the front of the semi-detached houses. "I haven't seen any washing on the line and wondered if everything is okay."

Is the absence of laundry on the washing line a definitive indication that something is wrong wondered JP?

"All's fine," JP told him perkily. "I'm off for a few days tomorrow." Deed done, he thought to himself. If all else fails, his nosey neighbour would be sure to tell Liza about their brief conversation.

"That's great," his neighbour replied. "Life's too short to waste our retirement just sitting around."

JP disliked, almost despised, the misuse of idioms, particularly ones that were clearly untrue. If life was too short, then why had he forgotten most of it? If we cannot remember each precious day, isn't life too long? Anyway, the phrase was in praise of art, not the brevity of life.

"Ars longa vite brevis," JP replied.

"Ars what, old man?"

"Art is lasting; life is short," JP explained.

The neighbour nodded. "Your daughter's place, is it?"

"Yes," JP lied and immediately regretted it. Why did he tell him he was visiting his daughter?

"It's times like this that you need your family, Jean." The pronunciation of John with a 'zh', like a soft 'g', was a reasonable but entirely unnecessary attempt at a French accent. Most people called him John, and his friends used his initials. His late father was the only person to call him Jean-Paul.

JP deposited the black sack in the dustbin and slammed the lid a little too heavily. Convinced that his neighbour did not have any children, he wanted to say something truculent but stopped himself from mentioning it. Enough insults had been discharged this morning.

"Yes, I suppose you're right," he answered, instead of "how would you know?"

"Shall I put the dustbins out front for you on Thursday?"

He just wanted to know whether JP was going to be back by Thursday. At least that's what JP thought.

"Very kind of you," came a smiling reply.

"I watched a bizarre film last night, Jean. *The Men Who Stare At Goats*. Have you seen it?" The neighbour reflected for only a second on JP's shake of the head before sallying forth with his wearisome resume of an equally tiresome film. "Bizarre it was, but absolutely true apparently." The monotonous drone continued on with a tale of soldiers who killed goats by staring at them.

A clamour of uninteresting information rattled from the nosey neighbour, leaving only milliseconds between each faintly linked sentence. JP pounced at the first tiny suspension in the man's diatribe about paranormal military practices in America. He shrugged his shoulders regrettably to indicate he had not seen the movie and, more importantly, to bring the one-sided conversation to a close. A reluctant smile and a sardonic "merci monsieur," and JP departed along the path by the side of the house to finish his packing.

Closing the rickety garden gate behind him, JP gazed sullenly at the lawn. The garden required attention, but time had to be devoted elsewhere. A rather ragged-looking herb garden stood by the fence, a somewhat poor attempt at growing Salerno basil. Planted with loving care by Rhonda's own hands, it flourished and filled the evening air with its scent for a little more than two weeks. The sprawling Bougainvillea and intoxicating aroma of Basil now summon him from a distant land, where she may be found shrouded midst that fragrance.

  It was time to finish packing. JP stared at the bed, and the open suitcase stared back at him. Goats, he thinks to himself as the clothes plead to be packed. However, JP's attention turns to the picture of his wife on the windowsill. "I'll need that," he tells himself as he recalls a forgotten task. He removes it from the frame and stares at her blue eyes glistening, almost tearful in a wayward look away from the camera. She gazes at some unidentified object or person, not wishing to kill her husband by fixing her stare upon him. She disliked having her photograph taken. JP made an awkward bow, but Rhonda always made an awkward pose. He returned to the bedroom to collect another tie.

From the doorway, his small study beckoned across the upstairs landing. Mission HQ, where he had spent recent days, or was it weeks, planning the trip. "No," he told himself, "it must have been several weeks." He picked up some of the travel documents. "Some of these are dated in May, and it is now June." But he doubted the evidence because he must have worn the shirts in that time. Perhaps he had ironed them after all.

The study contained maps, guidebooks, train timetables, pens, copies of email messages, sheets of printed A4 paper detailing timings, directions and hotel reservations. And next to them sat a new journal with its hungry blank pages eager to be filled with observations and anecdotes of the trip.

Close by, a separate collection of essential items formed a regimented column ready to advance on the enemy. A leather travel wallet, foreign currency, credit cards, boarding passes and railway tickets. The last two components were fanned out in chronological order. The trip would take three weeks to complete, and JP frequently wondered how much of it would be spent with Rhonda. Where along that winding pathway from the south of France to the Italian Lakes would he find her? The tickets and boarding passes had been ticked off against a list that rested next to them.

JP scrutinised the seven groups of documents and mouthed the words plane, train, bus, bus, train, train, boat. He corrected himself, muttered hydrofoil and went back to the bedroom to finish packing his suitcase.

He looked about the room, still lost in that thought about where he might meet Rhonda along the route. Her passport had gone and her mobile phone of course. Not that she was answering it. He looked at the open wardrobe noting which dresses were missing. They were there one day and missing the next. Rhonda was there one day, and then, she was gone. Clothes, passport, credit cards and suitcase. Rhonda's needs were the same as JP's. They always had been, and they always will be. Rhonda wants to be found, he convinced himself.

He crossed the room and stood gazing into the half-empty wardrobe. His clothes lay on the bed, and Rhonda's were somewhere unknown. He took in the evocative fragrance of her clothes that remained hanging in the cupboard. He wanted to bury his head in the treasured memories absorbed by the cloth and smell the joy embedded in each thread.

He tried again to remember when it happened, how long ago his wife had left. He was convinced he should be able to remember, but a torrent of emotion had swept away the details. This was understandable, he convinced himself. "Only to be expected," he told himself whenever it began to bother him. One moment she was there just like her clothes had been. And then.... And then she was gone. He just couldn't remember when that moment happened.

He and Rhonda were planning a holiday together, another holiday, not this one, not the one laid out on the bed. Those two weeks in Sicily were abandoned like the refugee boat he saw on the beach as he walked home along the promenade last week, unwanted, unneeded. JP had been attending local evening classes to refresh his grasp of the Italian language. He continued going after Rhonda left, although, at first, he knew it didn't make sense. If she had left, they wouldn't be going on a holiday. So why learn how to speak Italian? That is when the plan first came to him. That was the conception.

Uncertainty and strange omens obscured the interim, like the ironed shirts and the fish fingers. They never ate fish fingers in over forty years of married life, so why would she leave a packet in the fridge? And why didn't she answer her phone? It was clearly being charged up every day, so she was there, somewhere. Presumably, she didn't want to be found. But that wasn't going to stop JP from discovering her whereabouts. That was the object of the plan. That was fulfilment, the conclusion, finding Rhonda. JP could be self-willed, and this was a time to be stubbornly, relentlessly obstinate.

He spent his days planning the trip. 'If planning is not the whole of management, it is at least the greater part.' Before he retired from the sixth-form college, this Henri Fayol quote was used by JP for his first lesson each year. His father had quoted the French industrialist during his childhood. JP considered it a good starting point for any business studies course. By the end of year one, the content would become more philosophical. Planning might be the whole of management, but there was much more to it than that. All things being equal, someone gives their business to someone they like. All things not being equal, they still give their business to someone they like. It sounded like nepotism or something close to it. But JP could be pretty cynical. By year two, the phlegmatic became more theoretical. It was easier to accept that people have their own world of meaning that might be alien to ours. This was the degenerate nature of business. Not that JP had ever been in business. Those who can, do, and those who can't, teach.

On most evenings, when he wasn't attending Italian language classes, he would be out ambling between St Leonards and Hastings. It was his English version of La Passeggiata, a pastime that means so much more to Italians than just an evening stroll. He filled his days by booking flights and train journeys online. Scanning through hotel websites, trying to recall all the places they visited together, wondering which of them had become Rhonda's bolt-hole. Then, as the sun went down on the lengthening days, he would walk. Reflecting on the shoreline, thinking back, and suffering the anguish that accompanies such painful thoughts. Trying to remember when she left him became his own paradox riddle, and the answer is equally baffling. It must have been when he was with Mrs Rossi, learning the Italian verb to miss someone. Curiously it is mancare. Mancaro, mancari, mancara, mancariamo, mancarate, mancarano. JP missed Rhonda in every tense and every sense of the word. This wasn't La Passeggiata because they did that together. This was the loneliness of the mindless wanderer.

When using the promenade route, the homeward journey from college was more pleasant but a little longer. A torch was required during the winter term, but not in the early summer. The full-time students had broken up and only those regarded as mature students attending the adult education classes remained. Along the sea wall, he repeated some of the phrases he had learned that evening, talking quite loudly above the noise of the crashing waves. The boat he saw last week had been removed. Looking out to sea, he wondered how many people might be out there risking their lives in an attempt to find a new life. JP had no interest in finding a new life. He just wanted his old one back again.

Each time he returned to college in the weeks following Rhonda's departure, he felt a little more anxious than before. He convinced himself that this was when it all began. The nightmare started one moonless night. Rhonda left him one dark night while he attended his Italian class. She was gone when he came home from college. He hoped, against all logic, that this is how the mystery might end. One day JP would come back muttering, "mi manca mia moglie," and Rhonda would be there, and the nightmare would be over. Or maybe it was an actual nightmare, and soon he would wake up. She would be there again when he awoke from this woeful dream.

He rang the doorbell and stood gazing downwards, recalling how it once played a rudimentary version of Frere Jacques. The tune pleased his father and annoyed his mother in equal measure. They had both passed from this world some years ago, sometime between their two grandchildren arriving and Rhonda leaving. These had become the critical points, the watersheds of his lifetime. Now the doorbell played O solo mio - a measure of his independence from his domineering father who clung to his French heritage, just like those refugees must have clung to that boat on the beach.

Sometime between the arrival of his kids and the departure of his wife was actually 2004. His parents died in 2004. His father at the beginning of the year and his mother just two months later. Liza asked if her grandmother had died of a broken heart. Lester, as sarcastic as ever, told her it was probably the relief. Independence must have been an alien concept to a woman who lived under a domineering partner for her entire adult life.

JP found himself thinking more about his father lately. Dancing with the cache of childhood memories, recalling tiny elements of his essentially authoritarian character. He would gaze at photographs, desperately trying to both remember and yet forget different times in their relationship. The old man's love of the Charles Aznavour record *She* came to mind. JP laughed as he recalled playing the Elvis Costello version when his parents visited. The old man died a few weeks after that dinner party. And, in the days that followed, JP gathered up photographs, scribbled down recollections in his journal as if the act of doing so would lessen the loss. And, when his own memory began to fade, he clung to that wreckage with curious vigour.

Independence is overrated, JP told himself as he waited in hope rather than expectation outside the flat, believing Rhonda might open the door. The four syllables of the word independence pulsated and echoed like the pendulum of steel balls on the bank manager's desk when he visited recently. He couldn't remember why he called at the bank, but Liza was with him, so it must have been something to do with her.

He sighed, turned the key, opened the door and went over to the table to recover a notebook. He scribbled out his latest list of useful Italian phrases. Except it wasn't a scribble, it was neatly written. It would be transferred into the appropriate journal later, using his favourite fountain pen. But, for now, he had to get them down on paper in case he forgot. He forgot much more lately. Not when his parents had died, but things that happened more recently than that. Things like when he had ironed the shirts and the date his wife chose to leave him. He remembered her birthday, and he never forgot their wedding anniversary, so why could he not remember when she left. After all, it was more recent than the other dates.

Whenever JP and Rhonda planned a holiday to their beloved Italy, he would swot up on the language. It wasn't cramming. JP didn't even cram at school or university. JP lived up to his name Jean-Paul Preparé. He prepared for everything. And the first precursor to a fortnight in Sicily, Tuscany, Piedmonte or the Lakes would be the registration at local evening classes, refreshing his skills and exploring the vocabulary of the Romantic language.

"Where are you off to this year?" Mrs Rossi would ask at the beginning of each term.

Her classes presented an opportunity to develop the specific phrases he intended to use on his next visit. The tutor was used to his precise yet predictable questions about terms used in hotels or restaurants. JP didn't just want to order fish for dinner. He wished to converse with the owner on whether the fish is from the lake or what wine might best accompany a particular dish. This year, however, the questions were singularly uncommon. His questions were different, and the phrases he sought clarification on were more intimate. 'E il esce fresco da questo lago,' became 'un'estate Italiana recordi non condivisi.' An Italian summer of unshared memories. The terms were now suppliant pleas to an unnamed party rather than questions about the menu. JP would divide questions up to be reconstituted as complete sentences later.

"How does one say they cannot bear something, rather than they do not like something?" he asked the tutor. He knew 'non mi piace' was to dislike, he assured the young woman. She interrupted the lesson so that the other students might participate in what was becoming a one-to-one language course.

"It's 'non posso sopportare questo,'" she answered before moving on quickly. It was only later, before bedtime, as she brushed her teeth, that the enquiry made sense. She spat out the toothpaste and rinsed her mouth. And, gazing into the mirror, she mumbled "Non posso soportare questo un'estate Italiana recordi non condivisi."

Her voice was still loud enough to be heard by her husband, a man of Italian descent, who spoke fluent Italian. "You cannot bear an Italian summer of unshared memories?" he stuttered. "What on earth does that mean?" His wife shook her head. As she lay in bed, her thoughts rested on the sentence as her head rested on the pillow. She paused to regret how little she knew about her students.

As he lay in bed recalling that evening's lesson, JP repeated the words. "Non posso soportare questo un'estate Italiana recordi non condivisi," he whispered. "I cannot bear an Italian summer of unshared memories."

2

Antibes, Côte d'Azur

The homogeneous nature of airports makes one terminal identical to another. Such deception is the enemy of memory, and the armies of this particular adversary were taking the high ground. JP wondered when he had last been in this particularly uninviting carbuncle of architecture. Requesting an extra sausage in the noisy and unappetising restaurant was simply a device to make this visit different from the previous one. He had already idled away his time purchasing some shaving balm from a pretty young woman who was dressed for her first prom rather than working in a shop. He ambled around the bookshop and sighed at the airport lounge fodder that people found suitable holiday reading.

With the relentless harmony of moons and tides, an endless flow of bodies traipsed from check-in to the departure gate, pausing only temporarily at the duty-free shop or, like him, to consume a second-class breakfast to blunt the monotony of the ordeal. He subdued the throbbing overture of prattling voices by dreamily recalling such encounters from his youth.

"Seven guineas," he said aloud, startling a woman on the adjoining table. He pointed to the menu, which clarified nothing. He sat converting the price of his breakfast into guineas, the currency used for his first package holiday when the flying experience was a pleasure equal to the holiday itself. That almost forgotten privilege of café society, now vulgarised to the point of ridicule. He looked down at his empty plate and yearned for lake fish or fresh pasta. He paid the bill, left an obligatory tip, and strolled towards the departure gate number indicated on the illuminated message board.

'This is a pre-boarding announcement for flight BA932 to Nice. We are now inviting those passengers with small children and any passengers requiring special assistance to begin boarding at this time. Please have your boarding pass ready.'

Heedless to the absence of children and indifferent to the needs of anyone requiring help, everyone in the waiting area rose to their feet. Well, everyone except JP, who frowning at their stupidity, threw his arms in the air. Then, suddenly conscious of people looking at him, he stretched and faked a yawn. Perhaps they all have special needs, thought JP a little scathingly. He approached the departure gate only when instructed by a second announcement. The last passenger to board the flight required two passengers to vacate their seats so that he might occupy the window seat which he had reserved.

The aircraft wheeled around ninety degrees to the left and straightened up at the end of the runway. The seatbelt light pinged on and off. And the cabin crew strapped themselves in their seats at the front of the aircraft. There followed that familiar moment of mixed emotions. A cocktail of intense sensations is how Rhonda described it in one of her more poetic moments. The pleasurable anticipation of visiting some distant, romantic location collides with the zesty, bitter hint of acute anxiety. Newsreel of plane crashes flash through the mind like a tidal wave, then Concorde bursts into flames on the runway. A dismembered fuselage is listing on the ocean's surface before disappearing beneath the waves. The passenger urges their mind to focus on a fairy-tale sunset, lying on a beach on some remote island far, far away.

The deafening sound of roaring engines fills the cabin, and JP is forced back into his seat as the aircraft lifts off from the runway. With his eyes heavenward, he reaches out for Rhonda's hand, but it isn't there. The man in the adjacent seat snatches his hand away from the fondling fingers. He nonchalantly removes a magazine from the seat pocket in front of him.

According to the weather forecast, it was one or two degrees warmer in the south of France than in the south of England. But as he disembarked onto the aircraft steps, JP felt the smack of heat against his face. The humidity and the sultry airlessness of the day said welcome to a different land. There was an emptiness about the airport, which is impossible to find in England and the passengers filed through to a deserted arrivals hall. Passport control staff were amiable, and there were no queues at the taxi rank outside. The efficiency of his arrival served only to convince JP that the mission would be a success.

"Hôtel Sainte Valerie à Juan les Pins," he commanded in a rather contrived French accent.

"The hotel Sainte Valerie in Antibes, sir," the driver repeated in almost perfect English.

JP held no unrealistic expectations for stage one of his expedition. It took Stanley eight months to find Livingstone and his search party was two hundred strong. This intrepid explorer did not anticipate finding Rhonda in Antibes, but it was an excellent place to start. And he knew that if she were there, she would be staying at a particular hotel. This element of the mission would be a brief one.

Rhonda and JP stayed here about four years ago. And though it wasn't his wife's favourite holiday, it was geographically the most suitable location to begin his search for her. He was under no misapprehension of a breakthrough. The plan was to stay at Antibes for just one night because it would be apparent immediately, or at least by breakfast the following morning that Rhonda was not there. She extolled the peaceful ambience of the courtyard at the Sainte Valerie Hotel. A haven of peace, she called it, made perfect, it seems, by an unequalled breakfast.

If Rhonda is in Antibes, then she will be eating breakfast at Saint Valerie in the morning. So, on his first afternoon in Antibes, JP was a free agent with nothing particular to do. He decided not to loiter about the hotel in the faint hope of Rhonda appearing there. There was time to kill before dinner, and he was not one for sitting around the swimming pool or indulging in wasteful afternoon naps.

Once JP laid out the toiletries and medication in the bathroom, and the passport and travel documents were secure in the room safe, he went for an aimless stroll. He left the suitcase undisturbed other than to remove a pair of trousers, a shirt, a tie, some underwear and socks. With the items required for dinner dutifully placed on the top of his other clothes in the case, he paused for reflection. Planning was indeed the whole of management. He left the clothing hanging on the wardrobe and went out into the afternoon sunshine.

Thirty minutes later, JP found himself in the old town, wandering through its meandering alleyways. As he walked past the Picasso Museum at Chateau Grimaldi, he suddenly stopped, unable to remember how he arrived at this spot. He'd just been walking inattentively, sub-consciously following the footsteps of some previous ramble with Rhonda. He looked at his watch and set off along the promenade with its view of an ashen white pebble beach and the smell of the Mediterranean Sea. He arrived back at the hotel, still thinking of Rhonda, and went back to his room.

He shaved, showered and dressed for dinner. He looked at the tie a little dubiously at first but felt undressed without it. As he tied it, he stood on the small balcony looking around to see if Rhonda might be sitting by the swimming pool as she had been back in that hot summer of 2018. His wife wrung every ounce of sunshine from each sunny day before she dressed for dinner. There had been a campaign for a People's Vote at home to reverse Brexit, and President Trump had visited the UK. Both are obsolete issues now, although who knows?

Rhonda was not sitting by the pool, and a cursory forage around the hotel provided little evidence that he had found his wife at the first attempt. The disappointment was momentary, for he wasn't sure he wanted to discover her at the first attempt anyway.

As the sun began to take its leave from the day, he walked an easily remembered path towards the beach, turning right before the Avenue Georges Gallice reached the promenade. The New Orleans bar stood in a side street leading directly to the beach and attracted a little passing trade with live jazz performances on most evenings. Rhonda didn't particularly like jazz, but the tables outside provided entertainment on several levels. You might wish to indulge in some people-watching or just sit quietly and listen to the muted sound of live music from inside the building. Rhonda wasn't sitting outside the bar either, of course. But then, he didn't expect her to be. And yet, JP would have felt stupid travelling around Italy looking for his wife when she might have been in France all the time. He was sure of that. It was a box he had to tick on the way to more promising locations, places where Rhonda was likely to be hidden away, sitting on some balcony somewhere reading her Kindle. There would be other boxes to tick along the way too. But in one of those boxes, he would find her.

Shaded from the slowly declining evening sun was a choice of seats. More importantly, they were all empty, offering protection against intrusive strangers who may wish to start a conversation. JP had showered and shaved before he came out. His milky skin was one clue to his age, lacking the tautness of a younger man. And his fair hair, turning ash grey on the short sideburns that swept back over his ears, was another.

The musicians inside the building were warming up. Most holidaymakers were either at the beach or had returned to their hotels to change for dinner. Antibes is an expensive resort that does not attract the average tourist. Yes, JP thought to himself, visitors to Antibes are more inclined to change for dinner. Not a dinner suit, of course, that was a little further along the coast. Antibes was smart casual which, in practice, meant very few ties.

As he hesitated about going inside to order a drink, a waiter came out of the door and glanced towards him. JP returned the young man's somewhat laboured smile and picked up the menu held upright on the table by a small metal stand. It offered a plate of charcuterie for ten euros, but it was too early to eat. He knew what he wanted to drink, but a wave of the menu confirmed his intention to order one. He planned an evening meal later, so the choice was obvious. In any case, he had taken the trouble to learn how to order a gin and tonic in most European languages.

"Gin et tonique avec de la glace et du citron,"

"Bien sûr, mon plaisir monsieur. Quel merveilleux coucher de soleil. Restez-vous longtemps à Juan les Pins?"

Right, thought JP as he tried to unscramble the words that tumbled about in his head, the syllables welding together to provide a cacophony of sounds. He grasped at the grey, fading memories of his French lessons from school and restructured the sounds. Good, my pleasure, sir. So that's the G&T taken care of, but what was the other stuff. A marvellous couch in the sun. I have a nice seat in the sun? And, you rest a long time in Juan Les Pin?

"Juste jusqu'au diner," he finally answered before translating it into English to prevent the waiter from replying again.

He had learned Italian at evening classes and a little French at school, but not to the level that would enable a lengthy conversation. "Just until dinner," JP replied.

He took out his mobile phone to check for any calls, but there hadn't been any. He gazed at it pensively, pressing some keys and listening. 'Hi, this is Rhonda.' He snatched the phone away, took a breath, and brought it back to his ear. 'I'll call you back.'

The New Orleans bar was one of the best places for people-watching in Juan les Pins. Well, apart from the everlasting boule tournament on the beach, which generally attracted a capacity crowd. But there was nobody to watch. The street was empty. Le promenade, it seems, is a poor imitation of la passeggiata. Not a soul passed by until a young woman, perhaps thirty years old, approached from the beach. She wore a dress entirely unsuitable for the beach. Indeed it would not have looked out of place in the more salubrious resorts further along the coast. The young woman was glowing with health, and she moved towards him with smooth undulating steps, her heels clicking lightly on the pavement. Her eyes lit up as she saw him sitting alone, waiting for his first drink of the evening. She smiled from a distance, causing him to wonder if someone was sitting behind him. There wasn't, of course, and she paused in front of him.

"What a delightful evening," she said in good English. She clearly caught the end of his conversation with the waiter and witnessed him struggling with her mother tongue.

As the idea of responding in French tossed about in his mind, the young woman smiled pleasantly. "May I join you."

There was a joyful innocence about JP Preparé. Many of his former colleagues thought him an intelligent individual, although few people would consider him worldly.

The impious and profane had passed him by. So, when the young woman asked if he would like to buy her a drink, he took the suggestion literally. He may have been bemused by the nubile young woman's interest in him, but he could not conceal the pleasure he felt at having such prepossessing company on his first evening abroad. The start of what might prove to be a long and lonely journey in a foreign land.

"Mon Plaisir ma chère dame," JP replied, hoping that she might recognise his limited vocabulary.

The waiter appeared, carrying a tray containing a gin and tonic. The young woman seemed to recognise him and waved, much as the Queen waves with benign geniality, towards the tourists outside Windsor Castle.

"Mon habituel s'il vous plaît Albert."

JP's schoolboy French was sufficient for him to understand that she was ordering her usual drink and the waiter's name was Albert.

As the waiter returned casually back into the bar, the woman introduced herself as Chloe. Her blue eyes and golden tresses tumbling about her neck reminded him of Bridget Bardot. Chloe looked much younger than JP remembered the famous movie star, uncomfortably young in fact. She spoke good English and pursed her lips just like Bardot as she smiled, waiting for him to respond. JP was still wondering what interest such an attractive young woman might have in him. After his confusing dialogue with the waiter, he decided to speak English, but his answer came out in English and part French.

"Jean-Paul Preparé, at your service, mademoiselle."

"Oh êtes-vous français?" She hesitated, wondering if he really had a French surname or whether he was simply pronouncing it with a French accent. She translated her own question. "Are you French?"

"No, no," he insisted. "Well, not since the sixteenth century."

Chloe laughed out loud. "You don't look that old."

JP desperately wanted to ask how old she thought he looked.

He certainly didn't look like a man who would soon be seventy years old. But then, he was not young or handsome enough to attract a beautiful young woman. If she asked, he would diplomatically admit to being in his sixties although, in truth, he was about to fall from that particular age band.

She smiled, wondering if her companion was naïve or just enjoyed role-playing as many of her other clients did. Was he the type to insist she wore a nurse's uniform?

Or was he indeed one of life's pure and guileless individuals. It was the latter, she thought, although she was sufficiently street-wise to presume it was the former.

The young woman's forwardness was seen as nothing more than youthful exuberance by JP. He felt both fortunate and pleased to have company on the first evening of his trip. The young woman was probably waiting for her date to arrive and didn't want to sit alone. Sitting with a distinguished-looking gentleman, particularly an Englishman, should be enough to deter any aspiring lotharios.

Rhonda would think nothing of her husband being in the company of a young woman. Surprised, yes. But not threatened or annoyed for, unlike the scantily clad Chloe, Rhonda was entirely confident of her husband's innocence. In truth, Rhonda would be laughing aloud, wondering how her poor, uninitiated husband might escape such a compromisingly awkward situation.

The waiter returned with Chloe's drink, smiled a little too knowingly and placed the bill on the table. Chloe lifted the flute of bubbling champagne, tilted it towards JP and raised her eyebrows. The waiter stood still, expecting JP to settle his account. A little surprised, he rummaged in his pockets for some cash which he glanced at furtively. The note was a little over the amount but, waving his hand, he dismissed the waiter. Albert was not dismissed so easily, and he waited for something more substantial for his trouble. JP was still gazing into the young woman's eyes but soon became aware of the waiter's inertia. He pushed another banknote into the waiting hand, and Albert left. Quite why the waiter assumed they would not require any further drinks was occupying JP's thoughts when the young woman suddenly leaned towards him. Their cheeks nearly met.

"You have been kind enough to buy me a drink," Chloe whispered in his ear. "Perhaps you would like me to entertain you."

As she delivered her final two words, the world suddenly came into focus. A eureka moment seized JP's confusion, and an intuitive grasp of events took place. Awareness replaced apprehension on the old man's face. He leaned back in his chair and sighed aloud. Of course, it all made perfect sense.

"Oh," he beamed loudly, adding, "Yes, I would."

Chloe was a little overwhelmed by his sudden enthusiasm and bewilderment transferred from JP to her with a pathogen's leap.

Having realised that Chloe was the singer with the band, a broad smile filled JP's face, and he took Chloe's shoulders in his hands. "I bet you're absolutely brilliant at it, aren't you?"

His sudden forwardness alarmed Chloe, and her unease quickened further when JP removed his mobile phone and took a selfie of him with the lead singer of the band at The New Orleans Bar. Rhonda was going to be so impressed when he showed it to her.

JP checked his watch. "What time are you performing?"

"We'll finish our drinks first, shall we?"

JP nodded, and when that time came, Chloe asked if she might go back to JP's hotel room. She needed to freshen up.

"I imagine the facilities here are pretty poor, aren't they?" JP smiled.

Confusion passed from JP to the slightly bemused woman like a relay baton. She shrugged her bare shoulders.

"Afterwards," he exclaimed, "perhaps you would you like to have dinner with me?"

This time it was Chloe who looked at her watch.

"It might be quite expensive," she said.

"Why, where would you like to eat?"

"Let's just go back to your room first."

It suddenly occurred to JP that she might misconstrue his suggestion as a chat-up line. JP was a thoroughly reputable man, so affecting extreme politeness, he stammered. "Of course, of course. Let me show you to my room, and then we can get the evening started."

"Do you have any particular preferences?" she asked.

JP hurried through his list of favourite jazz classics in his mind. He raised his eyebrows and cast a broad smile in her direction, and declared his choice of song. "Anything goes," he announced.

Well, not quite anything, she thought as they entered an empty hotel reception. JP coughed politely to attract attention before obtaining the room key and leading Chloe to the first floor. He rejected the idea of explaining the situation to the clerk, who spoke good English, but the young man might still misinterpret events.

Now, though JP was undoubtedly naïve, he was not entirely absent of a suspicious nature. A stranger in his room presented many different possibilities of risk. And he was about to leave that stranger in his room while he visited the bathroom.

Perhaps he would then go to the bar while his guest showered, again leaving her alone in his room. So, as Chloe walked to the balcony and looked out at the swimming pool below, JP opened the room safe. He placed his credit cards and a mobile phone inside, keeping only a little cash on his person to pay for drinks when they returned to the bar. He then locked the safe again.

"I'd better just tidy the bathroom first," he suggested as Chloe waited by the door. The young woman surveyed the room, which had been serviced, and the bed made. There was no suggestion that the bathroom would not be in a similar condition. The true aim of the mission was not the cleanliness of the bathroom but the contents.

JP was self-conscious of the contents on display. Three different pills to combat high blood pressure, another to address itchy senile skin, together with medicinal creams and ointments, all portrayed a sick older man. And yet, JP felt nothing like that. These items would not convey his true self, so they needed to be removed from sight.

When JP returned from the bathroom, a sturdily built man confronted him. The tall man who was standing between him and Chloe held a large knife. He threw JP onto the bed, gave the knife to Chloe and began tying JP's hands. As he did so, the man instructed Chloe to check the room safe. She discovered, much to her friend's annoyance, that JP had locked it.

Few situations will cause a person to sober up quicker than a strange man entering their hotel room brandishing a knife with an eight-inch blade. JP assessed the circumstances in his usual methodical way. His first thought was to dismiss the notion that the degree of fear was in any way related to the size of the blade. This particular knife was capable of causing great pain and inevitably a gory death. A larger blade might only hasten the second stage, so it would certainly be no worse than the one flashing about his face.

"French?" the man asked.

"English," Chloe answered. Any pleasantness she had displayed earlier had disappeared, and her tone was now wholly distrustful.

She knew him, thought JP. She had let him in. The situation began to make sense to the old man.

JP was blessed with a logical, almost algorithmic brain, although Rhonda might not consider his pedantic manner blessed.

All situations appear as a recipe or set of instructions to him. There was a natural path to the solution of all problems. He remembered telling his wife as much on many occasions.

The results of specific actions can only lead to a finite list of reactions. JP's gift was to see those reactions as logical conclusions to an otherwise illogical situation. A strange man in his room brandishing a large knife was just another illogical situation on its way to finding a logical solution.

It was a desperate situation; there was no denying that much. The logical mind might conclude that this meant it would not end well. The fewer options available in any dispute, the more likely someone is to end up being disappointed. Or, in this case, murdered. And yet, JP was a pragmatic character, annoyingly so to his family and friends. Perhaps equally so for his enemies, too, although he had few of those. Here, however, in room 207 of the Sainte Valerie hotel, he had managed to find two enemies with a single purpose. Sometimes enemies arrive like buses, thought JP.

"What is the code to open the safe?" the man spluttered into his face. Droplets of spit striking JP's forehead.

The victim tried to relax and remained silent. And in the absence of a reply, his assailant waved a giant fist in front of the victim's face, instructing him, in broken English, to reveal the passcode. The silence continued, and the man pulled off a pillowcase and was about to gag his victim.

"There is no need to gag me," JP declared in an incredibly calm and patient voice. "I'm not going to call for help,"

"De ce? Motivul? Pourquoi? Why?" the man shouted, forgetting momentarily what language his victim spoke.

"Well," stuttered JP, wondering if he detected some Romanian in the man's questioning. "Because I don't need help."

"Why?" the man asked again. The calmness of the statement in such a dangerous situation bemused him.

"Because I don't need anyone's help. And, to be honest, I would find the whole thing a little embarrassing. For my part, the fewer people involved, the better."

The man looked at Chloe and was confused.

"The way I see the situation is this," explained JP in the same monotonous tone. "You two are either capable of torture and murder, or you are not."

The woman flinched at his honesty.

"If you're not capable of killing me, then I have little reason to tell you the code to the safe. For you will not kill me whether or not I reveal it to you." He paused. "On the other hand, if you are capable of what will be a gruesome, violent, bloody murder, then you will kill me anyway, whether I tell you or not. So I still have no reason to tell you the code." He had their attention. "However, the great benefit of the second option is that if I don't reveal the code and you kill me, then the Police will discover my body - and also find the contents of the safe. These include my credit cards, cash, and mobile phone, which contains a photo of Chloe sitting outside The New Orleans bar with me. Now," he continued, "as Albert the barman knew what Chloe's usual drink was, I assume he knows her quite well, and so the Police will have no trouble finding her. And, through her, they will find you too." He stared into the man's eyes to see if his assailant was trying to take in the logic of his rather protracted argument.

With his hands still bound, JP clumsily pointed at the man. "So, there we have it. Put the gag on me and get on with it."

His attacker continued to hold the pillowcase in his hands. He and Chloe stared at each other for a few moments, wondering what the incredibly calm old man might say next. The answer was revealed a moment later because it was becoming increasingly difficult to silence their victim.

"In my pocket, you will find a little cash for your trouble. Please take it and leave. I won't be telephoning the Police. I'm leaving in the morning, and I don't want to delay my holiday by helping the Police with their enquiries, as they say."

The man shook his head and said something in French to Chloe. She untied JP's hands and waited for him to hand over the contents of his pockets, 145 euros in cash. The pair decided to cut their losses and leave, trusting JP would keep his promise and not call the Police. They left the room, leaving the door open and traipsed away down the corridor outside. As they went, he could hear Chloe remonstrating with her friend.

"I could have got more than 145 euros if I'd let the old bastard screw me!"

"He screwed both of us," he muttered.

The following morning, a little confused by the events of the previous evening, JP made his way down to a damp courtyard garden. It was a haven of peace, just as he remembered it when having breakfast with Rhonda. He thought he remembered hearing thunder in the night, and the sky looked as threatening as the previous night. The charm of the Provence style building and the Bougainvillea mellowed JP's thoughts.

A hidden yet impetuous sun held every intention of burning the dampness from the day. JP tucked himself away beneath the Mulberry tree arbour in a romantic corner of the garden, and the fragrance of citrus fruits freshened the warm intimacy of the place.

JP was the first to appear for breakfast and the last to leave at the end of the service. He began with a coffee and followed it with a bowl of fresh fruit before ordering a freshly cooked omelette, deliberately prolonging the process as he observed arrivals and departures. Not having eaten the previous evening, he ordered extra toast and a second pot of tea.

He sat, grateful for a few moments of silence to run through his plan for the day. There had been no sign of Rhonda, so he would now move on to Italy.

JP sighed a little but remained pragmatic as he had not expected to find his wife here. Eventually, the cleaners arrived, and he showed them a photograph of his wife. They spoke no English and shook their heads suspiciously, wondering what motive the man had to search for this woman. The speculation soon spread to the kitchen, where the cleaners reported the matter to the manager. A few minutes later, that smartly dressed manager arrived and addressed JP in perfect English.

"Excuse me, sir, but you were making enquiries with some members of staff. May I be of assistance?"

The most likely answer to the question was no. The manager could not assist JP in his enterprise except by ordering a taxi to take his guest to Nice-Ville railway station. JP produced the photograph, and the manager examined it.

"This is a photo of my wife," explained JP in a resigned tone of voice. "We've become separated, and I've been unable to contact her by phone. She was supposed to meet me here."

Having heard the numerous rumours in the kitchen, the manager gave JP a suspicious look and shook his head. He had not seen the woman. However, he had heard the night manager's story of a prostitute visiting Mr Preparé's room the previous night. So he wasn't surprised that the guest's wife had taken herself off.

3

Nice-Ville to Cuneo

The heavy overnight rain eased to a light drizzle as JP tried to weave his way around puddles and faltering pedestrians towards platform number two. Romanticised by heart-rending goodbyes, railway stations never quite lived up to their cinematic image in JP's view. Of course, he was not a romantic in any sense of the word. He was too practical to be considered sentimental.

The unusually damp scene at Nice-Ville station was less Celia Johnson and Trevor Howard and more the Grand National of commuting. Crowds of people tripping over luggage, swerving through barriers and avoiding the crush of human life as they skip over the water hazard to catch a departing train.

He considered breaking the journey, although not on this particular leg, but a later one. Turin to Ferrara provided an opportunity for lunch in Bologna. Yes, he would leave it until the views began to lose their novelty. He loved Italy but found all types of travel punishing. It was rarely enjoyable and more often a price that needed to be paid, a trade-off against the overindulgence of hotel living.

'Attention, attention.' The public address system crackled and hissed. And JP could vaguely decipher the word 'Genova' before further crackling from the overhead speakers concealed an indistinguishable message, ending in the word Ventimiglia. The raucous noise of marauding passengers overwhelmed the rest of the announcement, which sounded like 'binaire deux au lieu de binaire six.'

A swift decision by JP to change platforms was induced primarily by the exodus of passengers sweeping down a set of stairs. Platform Two had emptied even before the crackly loudspeaker message ended. JP knew his train was heading towards Genoa, and he would need to change trains at Ventimiglia. The rest of the instruction included platform two, where he was standing, and platform six, which was presumably where everyone else was scampering off to in a hurry.

He glanced at his ticket as he reached the top of the stairs on platform six, tripping on the last step as he did so. He added multi-tasking to the expanding lists of issues that increased in difficulty with each passing year. Much to his relief, his seat was unoccupied. He was in no mood for an argument that might damage the Anglo-Italian accord.

Just after two o'clock, the train left Nice-Ville station and began the first leg along the coast towards Genoa. It was a journey of only eighty kilometres. Still, it would take three hours to shuffle across the French-Italian border to Cuneo, with two changes at approximately hourly intervals. The rain had moved easterly, and a bright sun caused JP to squint as he checked his watch. Before he reached the famous old Italian seaport, he would need to change trains at Ventimiglia and head north, through the sun-drenched Piedmonte countryside. He would then change trains again at Fossano for the last leg to Cuneo. It would be nearly eight o'clock before he arrived at his destination.

Chloe, her aggressive friend and the events of last night drifted about his thoughts. He speculated on the popular philosophical argument of whether an unseen event ever actually occurs. He concluded that such events happen but vaporise immediately. They are the product of the immediate present, not the chronicled past.

Anything unremembered exists only at that moment. JP decided to waste no energy fretting about the events of last evening. Despite what we see on our screens and read in books, he assured himself, very few people are capable of murder. Sometimes, JP's annoying logic could be reassuring, at least for himself. Nevertheless, he convinced himself that it was simply an unfortunate incident and one that should not be mentioned to Liza or indeed Rhonda when they eventually met up.

JP reserved a seat on the left-hand side of the carriage, facing forward, on the shaded side of the train. His attention to detail at the planning stage was painful to anyone other than himself. It was something he was aware of, although it did not overly concern him. But he was certainly conscious of how annoying his behaviour could be to others. And, in his younger days, he almost convinced himself that his pedantry would eventually cause Rhonda to leave him one day.

JP looked along the carriage, noting that most passengers had chosen to sit on the right-hand side. And, in fairness, from there, they could appreciate the sea view that ran almost all the way to Ventimiglia.

The metronomic click-clacking of the aptly named sleepers lulled JP towards the land of nod. These repeated short naps eventually caused him to set his alarm to ensure he didn't miss his station. He'd been dreaming about Liza, reflecting on how she looked like her mother. They shared the same blond hair and resigned temperament to life, although Liza worried a lot more than Rhonda. Lester was the opposite, laid-back but rebellious. And he had red hair, a feature that greatly pleased his grandfather. "Napolean had striking red hair," JP's father commented when Lester was born. The comment suggested he knew the military leader personally. It also advocated support for his first grandchild having a traditional French Christian name. Jean-Napolean Preparé perhaps thought Rhonda silently.

"You do know that Napolean descended from a Tuscan nobleman, don't you, Dad? He was Italian." Such goading remarks only began after JP married. A sign of his independence.

"What are you going to call him then, Jean-Paul? Garibaldi?" his father fired back.

"Actually, Dad, Garibaldi was born in the south of France."

"Discussions with your father on French and Italian politics rarely end well," Rhonda was to comment later. "The two nations enjoy a rather complex relationship. Much like you and your father, JP."

Still hungry from not eating dinner the previous evening, JP wandered along the train to find the buffet car. He eventually found a small bar in the front carriage serving panini with tea or coffee. The coffee was an insult to the Italian veneration of the drink. And the tea wasn't Earl Grey, but more a watery grey solution. He ate half of the panini and then had to search for somewhere to dispose of the remainder.

The final leg of the journey was an unhurried passage passing vineyards, olive groves and acres of dry open land. The pace suited JP, for he was in no hurry. And, in any case, Rhonda needed time to think. He didn't want to disturb her escape too soon, for to do so might produce the wrong response. His wife always needed time to get used to an idea, and to press her too quickly for a decision rarely had a suitable outcome.

Most people would probably hire a car rather than endure a long, three-legged rail trip. But JP could never be considered most people. He detested driving so much that it wouldn't matter to him if he had to change trains ten times, for he would never consider driving on holiday. And he would certainly never get behind the wheel of a car in Italy. If the winding, narrow roads don't claim your life, the psychotic drivers will, he convinced himself.

It was early evening when he arrived at Cuneo station. At the front of the pre-war railway station was an anonymous-looking bar with bright red seats adjacent to an empty taxi rank. JP found a seat in the shade. Having found the stuffiness of the train almost unbearable, he sat down and ordered a coffee and some water. He would wait until a taxi arrived.

The helpful waiter insisted that the Hotel Principe di Piemonte was only a short walk from the station. On his previous trip to Cuneo with Rhonda, they had flown to Pisa airport, so JP had no recollection of the railway station or its proximity to the hotel.

It was getting late, but he felt exhausted from his travels. As he sat there, his suitcase identifying him as a tourist, he tried not to close his eyes in case he fell asleep. His mobile phone stirred him into life. It was Liza. They named their daughter after Liza Goddard. Not that she looked like the TV actress, although they were both blond. JP briefly harboured designs to call the baby girl Marie Antoinette in a desperate and belated attempt to appease his father. But Rhonda was having none of it.

"How could we ever visit the Place de la Concorde without picturing our daughter's namesake kneeling at the guillotine?" commented Rhonda. "Anyway," she continued unhesitatingly, "you do know the charges against her included incest as well as treason, don't you? Not what you would call a role model."

And then Donna was suggested. JP had a soft spot for the old movie star Donna Reed. Not that Rhonda knew anything about her husband's fondness for the famous actress. His thoughts about the naming of his daughter forty years ago were disturbed by his phone buzzing loudly. The name Liza was flashing on the screen. He would finish the story later, recalling it at his leisure in a bar somewhere.

The longer, international ring tone surprised Liza. "Dad, where are you? Are you out of the country?"

"Sorry, darling, let me ring you back. I can't hear you very well."

"Hmm!"

How on earth did Liza know he was abroad?

She has the same gift of foresight that her mother has, thought JP. We should have called her Sybil, not Liza. Like the proverbial rabbit, JP froze, trapped in the headlights. He needed a few moments to compose himself. His daughter's fretfulness aggravated his self-reproach in uncertain situations.

Liza was one of life's eternal pessimists. She carried her father's agonies like stigmata, or what the Italians called the divine favours of St Francis of Assisi.

A foreign ringtone must mean something is wrong. Several possible scenarios spun around Liza's head, forming an orderly queue with the most horrendous at the front. She waited for him to ring her back. Did he mean he would call her back immediately or later? She tutted and reached for her book.

Not one for light reading, Liza was sitting in her garden, navigating the ten days of Boccaccio's *Decameron*. JP hid the copy of *Les Miserables* that her grandfather gave her for Christmas. Her father had introduced her to Italian literature during their annual holidays there in the nineties. She enjoyed the parochiality of its literary masterpieces. Each region or town in Italy has their hometown hero, a particular author who captures the essence of the area. Lake Como has Manzoni, Florence has Boccacio, and it would claim Dante too. But Dante's eternal flame flickered in Ravenna, his final resting place. And Sicily was Lampedusa, of course.

Liza had read them all, *The Betrothed*, *The Decameron*, *The Leopard,* and even *The Divine Comedy*. Firstly because of her love of prose and secondly as a necessary part of her degree course studies. She continued her studies in order to teach the subject at a sixth form college. Choosing the same profession as her father was not a coincidence.

As consecrated ground, there was not in extent sufficient to provide tombs for the vast multitude of corpses which day and night, and almost every hour, were brought in eager haste to the churches for internment. Boccaccio's harrowing account of the fourteenth-century plague rekindled the challenges of Covid-19 in the present day. Liza's fearful nature found no comfort in the fact that plagues had come and gone before, and life prevailed. Liza's glass was always half empty. Her father was just happy to have a glass. This one happened to have a gin and tonic in it. JP swished the drink around the glass, rattling the ice, wondering what to tell his daughter when he finally summoned the courage to ring her back.

His view switched from the glass to his mobile phone, and he sighed heavily. The 'Mmm' at the end of their short conversation worried him.

Liza was forty years old and unmarried. Sometimes her father blamed himself, recalling his favourite actress Donna Reed's most famous role in the Christmas classic, *It's a Wonderful Life* with James Stewart. In that other world created in the movie, didn't she become a spinster librarian? Apart from studying European Literature instead of Business Studies, Liza mirrored her father through school and university and then she began teaching her favourite subject at sixth form college.

Just like her father, Liza was examining her phone, waiting a little impatiently for him to call her back. And, at the same time, she remained lost in the book. It was the fourth day of *The Decameron* and the burden of discourse, as Boccaccio called it, fell to Filomena. It was the saddest of any tale the party would listen to during their sojourn at the villa outside Florence. She reluctantly closed her book and looked back at her phone. Perhaps she should call him again.

Itinerant musing is born of idle days and traumatic times. The world was still preoccupied with the pandemic, and Liza lay, immersed in the fears and unfamiliarity of this unwelcome stranger. Others had weathered the storm, but that storm had caused too much personal anguish to pass so easily for this young woman. She tapped her fingernails on the phone and waited. The delay was an ill omen as all things were in her life.

The schools and colleges had closed early, but this did not stop Liza from producing ideas for her lessons. Idleness made her uncomfortable. Feet up in the garden, reading of epidemics past, she glanced at her phone again and counted to ten.

The clumps of hardy bluebells under the trees at the end of the garden had long since died. The ancient hedgerows that shaded them turned green, and the trees followed this timeless procession. A landscape of sylvan charm edges inchmeal towards midsummer, but in many places around the world, human life continued to tumble agonisingly towards unending winter. The plague that emerged from the east buried so many, and yet disemployed words resurfaced. Words like transmission and cluster are accompanied by long-forgotten emotions, mortal, primal, visceral. The phone suddenly wrenched Liza from her worries.

"Hello, darling. What are you up to?"

"Are you abroad, Dad?"

"Yes. I decided to pop over to Calais to stock up on some duty-free." JP was disappointed at the result of his ten-minute brainstorming session.

"There isn't duty-free anymore, Dad. You're only allowed two dozen bottles of wine. Nobody does the booze cruise thing anymore. The saving doesn't cover the cost of petrol."

"Well, I just felt like a run-out."

"You don't like driving."

"No, you're right. The driving has taken it out of me. I might stay over for a couple of days, actually. The weather is lovely."

"Hmm! It's raining all over northern Europe."

JP was running out of answers, and he knew the 'Hmm' meant she didn't believe him. Liza used the same vocal sounds as her mother. Hmm, had a definite purpose in her vocabulary. As did Uh-huh, which meant agreeing. This particular sound wasn't used frequently by either of them. Then there was Um, an indication that she was thinking, and Mm when she was listening, generally with the intention of contradicting you.

"No, erm yes," he stuttered. "I know, but it's supposed to dry up later."

"Dad, are you okay?" The voice sounded concerned and slightly irritated. There was no accompanying sound for this, and the delivery had a somewhat apprehensive tone.

He wanted to ask her about something important, yet it felt like a betrayal of his marriage vows. Which was it? Love or honour? Did Liza know about her mother's affair? Surely she told her everything. JP didn't hate Rhonda because of her adulterous fling. He despised her a little but wasn't sure if it was because she told him about it or left it more than thirty years before doing so. And then he felt sorry for her, having to carry the burden of that reproachable memory around for years. She lived a lie for so long. For what is the difference between a lie and an untold truth? The yoke of each weighs the same.

"How's Robert?" JP asked, ignoring her question.

"Okay," she replied. And before she could continue her interrogation, JP fired another question.

"You are still seeing him, aren't you?"

"Mm!"

"Have you spoken to Lester lately?"

"Dad, what's going on?" It was her turn to ignore the question.

"Look, I must go, darling. I'm about to go into a tunnel."

Liza saw the allegory. Her father was indeed about to go into a tunnel. The signs had been there for weeks. She thought about calling her brother but instead returned to the Renaissance prose of *The Decameron*. However, she couldn't help thinking about her father. What was he doing in Calais? Although not supercilious, her negative outlook on life had been endorsed by the pandemic, of course. Everything she had feared materialised before her, but it was not a time to be anything other than generous. She opened the book.

Kindred notions collided like stars in a distant galaxy, unseen and unheard. Reading Boccaccio was simply hopeful foraging for reassurance, something about knowing your enemy. Or perhaps it was the misplaced hopefulness of Nietzsche's premise that loitered in some dark corner. That which does not kill us makes us stronger. She sighed despondently, for reading itself is not an action. Moreover, it is the sister of procrastination, and it felt unworthy of her time. She thought back to the pandemic's beginning when the government sought volunteers to assist an overwhelmed NHS.

It was a decision that would surprise her few close friends. Just like her father, Liza had a mild aversion to meeting people for the first time, a misoxenist rather than a misanthrope, more discerning yet easily mistaken for a shy introvert.

Liza was proud of her bravery. She overcame her fears and volunteered. Being averse to meeting new people, it was entirely out of character for Liza to tentatively embark on a discussion with a young man she had never met. Exceptional even in normal times, and those early days of the pandemic were anything but ordinary. These were the days of social distancing, but they were alone together in a room, ignoring the two-metre rule - a misoxenist's nightmare.

She didn't dislike everyone, just the people she didn't know. So, she avoided strangers. Trains, pubs, bars and buses represented the most significant challenge, especially in the suburbs, where swarms of senior citizens shuffle around between shop, home, the GP and hospitals, insisting on engaging in mundane conversation with anyone forced to sit next to them on a bus. It is much safer to travel by bus in the days of a pandemic. Liza immediately regretted that thought. The Covid-19 pandemic carried nothing but ill-fortune in its wake.

Liza felt guilty about the fondness she held for those difficult days. Despite the anxiety, the mayhem and the loss of life, something was gratifying about that time. She gazed at her phone, wondering if there was any way she could find out where her father was from the call. JP stared at his phone, fearing the same thing.

On its approach to the hotel, the taxi passed two cathedrals that JP had visited with Rhonda on their last holiday there.

For such a small city as Cuneo, two basilicas seemed to be at least one too many. The city was cleaner, brighter since his last trip. He noticed little as they drove through the main piazza. He busied himself studying members of the crowd, hoping to find Rhonda. It reminded him of Lester's *Where's Wally* books. JP decided to visit both the cathedrals because Rhonda had remarked on the fine architecture of the city's churches. He didn't expect to find her there. Still, just retreading the paths they walked together eight years before would provide solace from the gnawing discomfort he felt in her absence. Yes, it was eight years ago. Strange how he could recall each loving moment of that trip, yet he could not remember what happened last week or the week before. It was the year of phone hacking and another virus, Ebola. Not a year for learning lessons, thought JP as the streets darkened.

The sun had set by the time the taxi turned into a large piazza and drew up outside the Hotel Principe di Piemonte. And despite a short cat-nap along the way, JP felt tired and longed for something to eat and a good night's rest. He stepped from the cab and convinced himself that Rhonda was not here.

4

Cuneo, Piedmonte

Unlike those planes, trains, taxis and buses that deign to be punctual, sleep chooses its own time to arrive and depart. A consistency of silence and temperature are the only sustenance of its life cycle. Even sleeping alone, undisturbed by movement or sound, as JP and Liza were this midsummer night, made little difference. Morpheus gives only minor consideration to such concessions. Sleep defies the natural development of human skills, which in all other regards grow with practice and experience. Yet sleep falls out of love with its ageing tenant. The friend of the babe and infant becomes the enemy of the elderly. Only an uncluttered mind and a clear conscience can withstand the inevitability of sleepless nights.

Nightfall brought anxious thoughts of the three men in Liza's life. She excluded her brother from the group on the basis that Lester was beyond her parochial care. Her new boyfriend, who she had just enjoyed dinner with, and her weirdly behaving father presented a constant cause for concern. The third was not Lester, but a young man she met in the hospital just over two years ago, when Covid-19 was released into an unsuspecting world, and she began voluntary work. Each of the men contributed to her insomnia that evening, and each gave her cause for reflection. She looked at the clock. Saturday was turning into Sunday, and the only consolation was that tomorrow would provide the opportunity for contemplation.

Sundays were the busiest day at the local cemetery. Still, today, with the sky overcast and threatening, Liza found herself almost alone, sitting on a bench looking towards a row of gravestones. It seemed a good time to phone her father, but he continued to be unhelpful. She learned there was a problem with the car. There was an even bigger problem with his alibi.

"Nothing serious," he told her. "But I'll probably be here for a week."

Their conversation was as informative as the previous one. Liza didn't believe any of his stories. In the restaurant last night, Robert had suggested a possible explanation for her father's behaviour. That suggestion was taking on greater credence with every sentence her father spoke.

"Look, whatever you're up to, Dad, I want you to call me tomorrow or the next day at the latest. I need to know you are okay." She hesitated, but there was no reply. She had second thoughts. "No, listen, Dad, call me every day while you're away. I need to hear from you if I'm going to retain my sanity."

"Uh-huh!" he replied.

"What does that mean?"

"Sorry, darling, I thought you were fluent in non-lexical vocables." His daughter was the only person who didn't find JP's use of precision language annoying.

"Yes, for sure, Liza, I'll call you tomorrow. Err, with news of the car."

"I'm more interested in you, Dad," she sighed. "By the way, what is the password to your computer at home?"

JP realised the purpose of her question immediately. If he revealed the password, she would be in Ferrara or Mantua waiting for him when he arrived.

"I will need to look it up. I'll text it to you."

"Don't forget, Dad," she sighed as she ended the call.

The peaceful reflection Liza hankered for was becoming increasingly unsettling through her father's continued and quite obvious secrecy. She took a deep breath and walked forlornly between the rows of graves, thinking of that day she met the young man at the hospital. Trapped in a room with someone she hadn't met before. The only comfort she drew from the situation was the intuitive awareness that it was even more unusual for him to make the acquaintance of a stranger. The softly-spoken introvert was solitary, although not particularly shy, but undoubtedly self-effacing. They shared very little about themselves, not just at the beginning but at any time during their acquaintance. It was as if their everyday lives had been suspended, hibernating somewhere, not to be disturbed. They could be actors, playing out their parts in an altered existence.

With this inadvertent yet entirely congruous thought occupying her mind, she was astonished to learn he was an actor, albeit an unemployed one. He loved Shakespeare, apparently, which was another surprise. She believed him to be too young, too socially immature to appreciate the Bard.

Some people might consider him slow-minded or backward, which made the interest in Shakespeare all the more preposterous. He didn't speak of his employment much, although, in truth, Liza believed it to be no more than a pastime rather than an activity capable of producing an income. But, curiously, he spoke little of it, and small talk replaced it, filling the brief, but everyday moments they found themselves alone together, stripping off. Liza's father would have considered Ben a simpleton or some other such derogatory term. Yet who is to say he has less a life than anyone else? Genetic engineering might eventually remove his like from the world, and the world would be a lesser place for it, deemed better by the rationalists but, in truth, worse.

Social media was a variety of practical and useless material during the first lockdown, so there was no shortage of topics to discuss. Jokes were spreading on Twitter as quickly as Covid-19 on the London Underground. There were the daily press conferences, Thursday's clap-for-our-carers ceremony, Trump, Boris,

Captain Tom, of course, and opinions – mainly those of other people, because neither of them held strong views about anything. What are the best three movies by the same director? Name as many books as you can with a colour in the title. Life became a parody of the TV game show *Pointless* because life itself became pointless. If you weren't human, what animal would you be?

He said that she would be a cat, which made her feel comfortable at a time of significant discomfort. He was a butterfly. She didn't tell him so, of course. Not that he was a colourful person. He was a transparent butterfly with a personality made of gossamer. What you see is what you get. A fragile individual whose emotions fermented in a darkened room, a young man who expressed few opinions. He did not wear his heart on his sleeve. He didn't need to because his emotions were not lines or creases upon his face but sentiments that rested in the nuance of his voice.

His name was Ben. She wasn't sure what his surname was. He told her once, but she didn't always understand his soft, murmuring tone, and she didn't like to ask again. It could be Henderson, or Anderson, though it might just as easily be Endersleigh or Anderton. Ben was like the Covid-19 disease itself: she didn't notice his arrival; his voice was soft and unvaried like a repetitive cough; she breathed differently in his company and, when it was over, the world had changed.

Ben avoided speaking about himself for ten days and, instead, told her tales of his inept uncle. Ben had interests of his own, of course, but he chose not to speak of them, not even his love of Shakespeare, which felt strange because Liza thought he might be on the spectrum even at this early stage of their relationship. And, rightly or wrongly, she had convinced herself that autistic people are prone to talk incessantly about their pet subject. But he didn't, so he probably wasn't autistic.

But there was something strange about him. He was out of step with the world, offset from humanity by a couple of degrees. He seemed less eccentric than conventional, stranded like a chrome ball in Newton's cradle, bouncing between the two. Neither Feste nor Trunculo was he, yet he possessed elements of wisdom and foolishness. He reminded Liza of her father, and she felt strangely guilty about having that thought.

On the day they met, he began a conversation about medical research into Covid-19. An anecdote, rather than a story, something he had read in a newspaper or seen on TV. Then, each day he told another tale and, by the fourth day, she was left wondering whether he was acting out scenes from *The Decameron*, reciting his daily story, which was almost always about his uncle. Indeed, only the first short anecdote about research and the tenth one, about funerals, were not on the recurring theme of Uncle Bob. Each day produced a story less likely than the one before. Tales of dreadful job interviews, failed career moves, and misguided actions. At one point, Liza thought his uncle might be a substitute for himself, as in 'a friend of mine has an embarrassing rash'. But Ben was too transparent to even consider such deceit.

Ben was a lonesome, though not a lonely individual, although he had no friends that he spoke of, and no family, having lost his one remaining relative, the much-loved Uncle Bob, in the first few weeks of the pandemic.

At the end of the second day, Liza and Ben were sitting together, waiting for the hot, damp sweat to drain from their bodies, and he told her one of the many stories about his uncle. The following day, Ben continued his compendium of stories with no mention of his own, presumably mundane existence. Self-isolation is of no consequence to someone whose life has been founded on social distancing. He wasn't the misanthrope. It was others who avoided him, deterred by his expressionless face and wary of his unconventional behaviour.

It troubled Liza a little, wondering why Ben never told anecdotes about himself. They were only ever about Uncle Bob as if Ben himself had no real life worth commenting on. By the fifth day of their acquaintance, she felt an urge to uncover some information on Ben, some morsel however insignificant. When she inquired, he simply returned to the subject of his uncle. The incredibly inept man apparently went to an international rugby match in Rome. It transpired he attended the game dressed as one of the three tenors. Liza suggested that, by definition, there should be three of them. Ben nodded, explaining that Bob had been let down by two friends, and went on to tell how his poor uncle was continually ridiculed by the crowd, who kept singing the theme tune from the Go Compare advert.

Liza never learned anything about Ben's work. He never spoke of the roles he had played or the theatres he had acted in.

She recognised her own insecurities in Ben, of course. And she began to see the reflection of her own shallow existence in the imposed lockdown. She mistook separation for privacy, her detachment from the world was actually confinement, and the seclusion of her own space was self-imposed solitude.

Before meeting Ben, she spent the first week of that lockdown at home, drowning. It was harvest time for the soothsayers and conspiracy theorists. Seven interminable days of quarantine, shopping online and exercising in the living room. She was counting the days but decided to make the days count. So she walked away from the ambiguities of government loans and support networks and marched towards the more critical issues of ventilators and personal protective equipment. She volunteered, and it was here, in the hospital, that she met Ben. They had nothing in common. If this was a dating app, he would be off her radar. Wrong age profile, unemployed, poorly educated, no shared interests, or few interests at all, with the obvious exception of his vaguely compelling uncle. They came from different backgrounds, held differing beliefs. They had nothing in common, except they worked on the same shift. They both volunteered at the same time and began their duties as hospital porters on the same day. They stripped off together in the sluice room and drank coffee to keep each other awake.

Their first conversation should have been a warning to her. Ben was convinced that doctors were using gnomes to find a cure for Covid-19. It soon became clear that the TV report he had seen was referring to genome research.

So she tried to correct him.

"No," he replied assuredly. "You don't pronounce the G in gnomes. The G is silent."

Liza stifled a grin and chose not to correct the young man. It seemed to her that a man gets an idea into his head, and it has nowhere to go. Women, even misoxenists like she was, tend to share it, for it is beyond their nature to keep it to themselves. And in exchanging it, the idea either dies or survives, much like the patients she had been wheeling around the hospital.

They both lost interest in the world, taking residence in a new universe where age, background, beliefs, and education had little relevance and meaning. Barely a day went by when a patient did not die from the disease. The much-promised flattening out of the Coronavirus spread came, followed by the downward curve which the experts had predicted. The pair lost interest in their insular world and became lost in another one.

Suddenly, the end appeared, or rumours of it, not in the shape of the Reaper, but like a sunrise over a recognisable landscape, filled with fading bluebells, white-blossomed hawthorn and full-leaved oaks.

Having the same shift, Ben and Liza shared the same rest days. So, after nine days on the trot, they took themselves off to the funeral of a patient, an old lady with no relatives. They were given special dispensation to attend, having met her briefly in hospital. It was good for Liza to see Ben outside the all-enveloping environment of the hospital.

It was no wonder that Ben enjoyed reading and acting the plays of Shakespeare, for the Bard was the only writer to pay homage to the fool on the hill, those who create advantage from adversity. His writing shone a torch on the wisdom of the simple-minded. Ben was such a painfully innocent individual, she thought to herself.

Liza didn't see Ben that morning. She arrived for her next shift the following week and didn't pay much heed to his absence. Why would she? Volunteers came and left in quick succession, few of them realising the steadfast commitment and energy required.

In truth, she never saw him again, apart from a glimpse on the isolation ward, where she delivered a patient three days later. Ben died four weeks after they met, having fallen victim to Covid-19. There was an empty space in her heart which she had been unaware of, and it had been filled for a short time by that strange young man. And now, it would remain occupied forever by his memory.

Liza placed the flowers on the grave, pondered on their posthumous existence and began walking back to the cemetery gates.

All things to end are made. Life and plague alike, fondness and fear, admiration and desperation. And the last of these to pass shall be love.

When she got home from the cemetery, Liza lost no time calling her brother, although, in fairness, he took twenty-four hours to return that call. And, in the meantime, she had heard nothing from her absent father.

"Where have you been, Lester," she asked in an agitated tone. "I've been calling for days." Omitting the number of days was a deliberate step to rouse any feelings of guilt. Lester didn't do guilt and had very little to do with feelings either, guilty or otherwise.

"Chill out," was his usual response to accusatory comments from his younger sister.

"Dad's gone to Calais to get some duty-free, so he says."

"Oh," came a surprisingly spontaneous reply. "Can you ask him to get me some Old Holborn?" Liza was speechless. "Do you know it's about fifty pence a gram now? That's more than cocaine," her brother added, unaffected by her gasp at the other end of the line.

"It's obviously a lie," Liza sighed, ignoring his stupid request.

"It's true! Forty quid for a small pouch of rolled tobacco. Unbelievable."

"I'm talking about Dad going to Calais," shouted Liza. "I was around his house a week ago, and he's stacked up with wine. He has a case delivered on standing order, but he hardly drinks the stuff without Mum around. So, he probably isn't in Calais."

"So?"

"So? So, where is he?" She didn't wait for an answer. "Anyway, you shouldn't smoke. You must be the only smoker left in the world, certainly the only one smoking roll-ups."

A lament of a sigh could be heard from the other end of the line. Liza ignored it and waited for her brother to speak. "Are you still seeing that doctor bloke?" he eventually asked, trying to deflect the conversation.

"He's not a doctor bloke, Lester. He's an orthopaedic registrar at the local hospital. He'll be a consultant surgeon in two years. Actually, I've been seeing him for a year and six weeks now."

"Yeah," came the dismissive response. "Stick your status on Facebook, and I'll give it a read."

"I don't do Facebook."

"Why are so many people in denial about Facebook? Everybody is just looking. What are they? Voyeurs?"

"I don't do it," Liza answered. "Can't be bothered with it anymore."

"Yes, that's what everyone says, so why are there three billion people on it?"

"Look, I'm going to Dad's house. I don't believe this Calais nonsense. I've got a key, and I'll have a look round. I'll give you a call from there tomorrow."

"Cool!"

"Anyway, are you seeing anyone?"

"It's complicated," her brother confessed.

"Is that your Facebook status then. Because you know there is a status on Facebook – It's complicated."

"I thought you didn't do Facebook. Anyway, I thought you popped round to Dad's house every week."

"Mm! There wasn't anything untoward when I visited last week. Dad wasn't there, so I just dropped some shopping off."

"Shopping, what shopping? You don't drop shopping off round my place."

"Food. We need to make sure Dad eats properly." She used the royal we, as she knew Lester had no intention of participating in her charitable work.

"Like what?" It sounded as if he hoped to be put on her list of charitable recipients.

"Food for him to eat. Last week I left some fish fingers." She paused, wanting to tell her brother something but knowing he would object. "I've taken some of mum's clothes too."

"You took her clothes?"

"Well, I made a start, yes, and her passport."

"Her passport?"

"Yes."

"Why?" laughed Lester. "She's not going anywhere."

Liza ended the call abruptly to show her disgust. Lester was the only person she could put the phone down on without feeling guilty.

Her brother was a thick-skinned and annoyingly lazy individual in her view. Invariably unemployed, he referred to himself as a seasonal worker. That seasonal work varied from hospitality to fruit picking. More recently, he had been a Safe Sleep Worker for Hastings council for a few weeks. The most prolonged period of work was spent as a Team Leader in a Christmas Grotto at the local department store. He wasn't keen on customer-facing positions and preferred the outdoor life of picking strawberries.

At first, JP was surprised to receive a text from his son. He couldn't remember the last time he received any communication from Lester. If JP wanted to speak with his son, it usually fell to him to make the call. However, when he read the content of the message, it was evident that Lester had spoken with Liza. Not having seen cigarettes for sale in a shop for several years, JP hadn't realised you could still buy rolled tobacco. He felt like addressing the request with the same sincerity of Lester's promise to repay his father for the Old Holborn when they next met. JP spoke less and less about his itinerant worker of a son. Rhonda called Lester a Lotus Eater, which was a little fanciful in JP's mind.

JP intended to spend only two nights in Cuneo before travelling further north. He and Rhonda had spent several holidays in the Piedmonte province. It was less popular than Tuscany, and they preferred undiscovered Italy. Cuneo and Saluzzo presented opportunities to practice his language skills, unlike Rome or the Lakes, where everyone spoke English, generally with an American accent.

It was late morning and JP, wearied by the relentless sun, decided to find a bar for an early glass of cold white wine. Beyond the town, the Alps and Po River created an unchanging landscape. The vineyards lay like a patchwork quilt across the hillsides, sustained by the

Gesso and the Strura di Demonte rivers that flow through those valleys and meet in the town. The towers and castles of Cuneo stand as witnesses to the history of this land. The fortified renaissance town, shaped and named after the word wedge, has an extraordinary austerity about it. And nowhere was this more evident than the Piazza Galimberti. It's a market square on Tuesday's but today, just a charming setting, with the bells of its fifteenth-century church inviting the faithful.

It was a struggle to find an empty table where he would not be expected to eat a full meal. It was too early to eat anyway. What he wanted was one of those hospitable Italian bars that supplement a glass of wine with a complimentary plate of savouries, olives and nuts. He wandered, getting increasingly tired until he came across a completely empty bar. The owner, an elderly woman, approached. He cast aside any worries of Norovirus and took a seat, placing the photograph of his wife on the table. "Buongiorno, quello che posso ottenere."

JP was hoping for a more leisurely start to his first direct tête-à-tête conversation. He ordered a glass of white wine in Italian and was pleased to see the woman understood him completely. She returned with a suitably chilled but somewhat small glass of white wine and an even smaller bowl of green unpitted olives, complete with one cocktail stick.

"Are you from London?" she asked in perfect English.

"No, I live on the coast, in the south of England," he answered, prodding an olive with the stick.

"Hastings." He considered adding that it was made famous by the Battle of Hastings. But then he thought she might not understand the significance of a skirmish that happened a thousand years ago in a foreign land.

"East Sussex," she said confidently. "I had a café in London for forty years."

JP sighed with disappointment. He had travelled across Europe only to sit in the one bar owned by someone so anglicised that she almost spoke with a Cockney accent. She introduced herself as Mrs Vacari and explained that her husband had died two years ago.

"I returned to my family in Cuneo with enough money to buy this bar."

The woman loitered by the table, wanting to make conversation. No other customers joined them. The pair couldn't have attracted less interest from the passing trade if they had been lepers. That passing trade was almost exclusively Italian for Cuneo attracts few tourists. Locals, it seemed to JP, prefer to sit at authentic Italian cafés.

But JP was nothing if not gallant, although mild-mannered would be more accurate. And he was undoubtedly too courteous to depart and leave the poor woman to suffer the ridicule of people cold-shouldering her.

When he finished the first glass, she brought out a bottle and another glass for herself. It became impossible to leave. She didn't sit down at first, but this changed when she spied the photograph. The woman stabbed her finger at it. But before she could ask, JP remembered the object of his travels.

"It's my wife," he announced. "We seem to have got separated, and I'm trying to find her."

The woman picked up the photograph and examined it closely.

"You got separated?"

JP couldn't be bothered to invent another story about his wife's disappearance. Instead, he confessed it all. His wife had left him without providing an explanation. He was sure she had travelled to Italy. Her passport was missing, along with a suitcase of clothes. He thought she may have gone to Cuneo. They had visited here eight years ago, and Rhonda loved it here. It was so typically Italian.

"A lost treasure," she called it.

"Why did she leave without you?"

"I don't know."

"Did you have an argument?"

"No."

The woman raised several other possibilities, during which time she had topped up her customer's glass several times and was now sitting opposite him. She wouldn't have noticed if a customer had arrived.

By the fourth glass of wine, JP had relieved himself of his innermost thoughts. Not only did he reveal how his wife had left him without even leaving a note, but also that he feared she may have chosen to revisit an old flame.

"She had an affair, you see," he told her. "Many years ago, of course."

He couldn't remember exactly when it happened. Nor did he know the name of the lover who shared the adulterous liaison, as he called it. And he certainly had no idea why Rhonda felt the need to take a lover. However, he felt convinced it was this long-forgotten affair that was behind her departure.

"Not long-forgotten by your wife," suggested Mrs Vacari.

"Quite," he answered in a resigned tone, before switching to Italian, in the hope of some practice. "Certo. sembra che l'amore non muoio mai," hoping it translated to 'Certainly. It seems love never dies.'

"La malattia Italiana," Mrs Vacari muttered.

Her time in England had made her Italian easier to understand, and JP had sufficient grasp to translate two or three-word statements. She spoke of an Italian disease, explaining that adultery is Italy's ailment. She rolled her tongue around the letter 'L' as if it was a syllable, "al-ler-menta." At first, he thought she said hell's lament. The woman switched unhesitatingly to English. She instinctively recognised that the weakness in JP's knowledge of the Italian language was his comprehension. He spoke it quite well, but his interpretation was flawed. The woman explained that betraying your business partner, boss, or colleague is the greatest sin in Italian culture, citing Judas and Brutus. But to commit adultery, to betray your wife, was the least of man's sins.

"Men are such fools that they cannot see there is little difference between the two. If a man can betray his wife, he can undoubtedly betray his business partner or friend".

She switched to English and back to Italian, and each sentence grew in length. But he recognised most of the words. The English word comfortable was separated into individual syllables again, so it was heard as 'come for table'.

"They are entirely com-for-table," she said, "to take a man as a partner who has betrayed his wife. They are unconvinced of the possibility that he will do the same to them."

After another hour, two passing women recognised Mrs Vacari and began talking to her. JP saw his opportunity to leave, but politeness prevented his escape. Soon it was too late. Mrs Vacari had found two extra glasses from an adjoining table, and his drink was refilled. She soon appraised the other women of JP's predicament, and the scene took on a drama with the emotional depth of a Puccini opera.

"This man has lost his wife. He thinks she has run away to Cuneo," the taller of the two women said to her friend.

"Che sarebbe scappato a Cuneo?" the friend questioned.

"Speak English," demanded Mrs Vacari. "This man understands little Italian. Make him feel welcome, for his wife has deserted him."

"Who would run away to Cuneo?" asked the second woman again. "Has she lost her mind?"

"Why did she choose Cuneo?" asked the tall woman. "Tell her to go to Turin. There's work there and some good-looking men too if she wants to have an affair."

"She doesn't want to have an affair," answered Mrs Vacari.

"No, she's already had an affair," remarked the other two women in chorus.

JP felt the need to speak up in his wife's defence. "She was the love of my life," he ventured a little meekly.

A fourth woman joined the group, along with a road-sweeper and two old men enjoying a lunchtime version of La Passeggiata.

"You can't have been the only love of her life," commented the road sweeper. "Did she have friends?"

"Some," answered JP. "Women she worked with, but nobody special."

The man looked unconvinced. His doubtful expression caused JP to think about it. Rhonda and a nice glass of wine, thought JP. Now there was a love story. But his unspoken thought caused him greater anguish, making his wife sound like an alcoholic. The advice came from all quarters, and JP found himself praying that Rhonda did not come round the corner and witness the assassination of her character.

"What do you regret?" asked one woman.

He looked confused by the question.

"In your marriage?" she clarified. "What do you regret?"

"There is nothing to regret."

"Then why did she leave?"

Shrugging his shoulders, JP placed the photograph back in his jacket pocket. He decided to take his leave, realising that he would only be in Cuneo for one more night and unlikely to see her again. Then he waited until Mrs Vacari next went inside for another bottle, and, seizing his opportunity, he strolled off.

JP looked around the café. He arrived thinking that the poor woman had few friends and even fewer customers. Now ten or twelve people were sitting and standing about the bar in that small piazza. Generously leaving a one hundred Euro note under his half-empty glass, he staggered out of the small piazza back towards his hotel.

The Italians have standards. Support the real Italians, rather than those who choose to spend most of their life in London. Misguided ideals are easily corrupted by a complimentary glass of wine and some gossip. Everyone, it seems, is looking for something that cannot be found.

After he had slept for an hour, he awoke to feel hungry and hungover. He decided to eat and have an early night. He needed to catch a bus to Saluzzo in the morning, and he was not looking forward to the journey. His initial instinct had been right. Rhonda was not in Cuneo. Another box had been ticked, another possibility exhausted.

5

Saluzzo, Piedmonte

Armed with shopping bags, crowds gather and scatter with hurried unease around the bus stop in Cuneo. Set amidst a wagon train of stalls in the market square, its position is convenient for shoppers, but for tourists like JP, the location presented problems. Shoppers arriving late for the market disembarked, as those early birds now seeking their transport home swelled towards the emptying bus. Both groups were consumed by the town dwellers taking to the streets for their weekly shop. Hither and thither, people rushed, tripping over JP's suitcase, which he dragged behind him on his slow journey through the impatient crowd. There is no natural directional flow. There is little scuttling about, just the noisy clatter of humanity rushing to avoid life itself.

JP was unsure if this was the right bus. He prayed for a helpful announcement of some kind. Unlike the variety of dialects spoken in Italy, JP found most public announcements easily understandable. The one advising a platform change at Nice-Ville Station had rather thrown our intrepid traveller, but that was in French, he assured himself. Today there was no announcement, helpful or otherwise.

Bus stops, airports, and railway stations are circles of Dante's Hell. Passengers arrive and depart without the segregation in those more coordinated places of worship to the gods of travel. Passengers scurry in all directions, and there is no place for an indolent traveller, such as JP. The romantic heritage of coaching inns and horse-drawn carriages is unrecognisable as the poor man weaves his way through the throng of shoppers caught up in the chaos.

A young man brushed past him and shouted above the crowd. "L'autobus per Saluzzo parte in cinque minuti."

JP reconstructed the words in his mind, translating the critical comment. The bus from Cuneo to Saluzzo would depart in five minutes. "Thank you," he told the young man, who was now lifting up JP's suitcase to carry it. For a brief moment, JP thought he was about to run away with his luggage. However, the crowd made it impossible to run anywhere, even without the added burden of carrying a large suitcase.

"Ti aiuterò," the man said.

"Thank you," JP repeated.

"I help you," the man repeated, realising that JP was English. Then, making his way through the crowd, with JP close behind, he threw the suitcase into the luggage compartment of the bus. JP was already rummaging through his pockets for some cash to reward the helpful stranger.

"No, no," the man insisted.

It wasn't until that point that the two men came face to face, and JP realised that his guardian angel was a priest.

"The greatest act of charity," continued the young man, "is the one that cannot be repaid."

The sluggish tottering progress of the bus on a constantly uneven surface caused passengers to sway. However, JP seemed out of sync with the others. The ageing bus's rattling suspension and noisy gear changes made the train to Cuneo look remarkably efficient. JP regretted ignoring the advice in the guidebook when he was planning this part of the trip. Unless you have a truly compelling reason to use a bus service in Italy, such as a strike on the train system, a train is by far the better option. This particular bus trudged slowly up and down hills, around sharp bends, teetering on the edge of destruction. There was no air conditioning, and the humidity was unbearable despite the windows being open. One young woman held a miniature battery-operated fan in front of her face. Others waved whatever they had in their hands.

Stopping at each small town and village on the way, the bus journey took less than one hour but seemed much longer. Exhausted by the conditions and unused to such frequent episodes of travel, JP dropped off to sleep at one point. He awoke to the sound of grumbling voices in the seats ahead of him. From his knowledge of the Italian language, he could make out that they were complaining about the bus service. One commented that the train service from Cuneo to Saluzzo had closed a couple of years ago due to budget cuts.

"Dov'è Mussolini quando hai bisogno di lui?" a woman asked.

JP smiled because he could easily translate her disgruntled expression. 'Where is Mussolini when you need him?' There was no answer to that question, of course. Nor was there an answer to his own, as yet, unresolved question. Where is Rhonda now that he needed her?

The views of the surrounding countryside improved dramatically as the bus approached the hilltop town, or rather the hillside town of Saluzzo. But he was relieved to eventually step down from the bus. It was only a short walk to the hotel, and the sun shone brightly from a cloudless sky. And yet, it was another day of regrets for JP. His thoughts remained tortured by the malign comments he made at the bar in Cuneo. Those ill-chosen comments about his wife's affair fermented in his mind during the tortuous bus ride, held firmly in place by a hangover.

Rhonda told him about the affair only a few years ago. According to her belated confession, it happened many years before she finally felt the need to tell her husband. She didn't say when it was, just that Lester was small. JP didn't want to know the details – not when, where, why, and certainly not who. He told her so at the time, denying her the cathartic cleansing of her soul. But he couldn't help reaching certain conclusions. She only mentioned that Lester was small, which suggested that Liza was not born yet. They married in 1977, and Lester was born the following year. Liza arrived in 1981, so the affair must have happened in 1979 or 1980. Once this approximate date was fixed in the victim's mind, he couldn't help speculating about where it happened. Sometimes, in moments of weakness, he thought about who the culprit might have been too. So despite his agonising overtures to the contrary, a part of him needed to know the truth about the affair. He just didn't want to hear it from Rhonda. He told her so quite fervently at the time, preventing her from going beyond how she had let him down. How she had allowed this man to take advantage of her. "We'll not speak of it again," he told her firmly.

His mobile phone rang just as he was putting it on charge in the hotel room. Still lost in deep thought about Rhonda, the sound made him jump.

"Dad, what's going on?"

"Nothing, darling. What do you mean?"

"I think you should come home, so we can talk about it."

"You're right, as usual, just like your mother. But I'm perfectly alright. I'll stay for a little longer. I'll ring you in a couple of days."

"Mm!" she murmured, or was it hmm! JP couldn't be sure if she was about to contradict him or whether she simply didn't believe him. He waited for her to speak again.

"Just talk to me, Dad. We need to talk about this."

The weather had got him into trouble previously, so he tried to think of some other mundane issue to discuss.

"Your mum stopped going to the gym, you know."

"Did she?"

"Yes, she was suing them."

The statement secured his daughter's attention.

"Mum? Suing the gym? Why?"

"I don't know."

"Well, did she have a fall? You have to be careful about these no win no fees insurers." She hesitated. "Or did she have concerns about Covid? Did Mum say anything about the safe practices at the gym?" Liza searched for something to ease her own guilt.

"I don't know. I just heard your mother speaking about it on the phone."

"Well, it doesn't matter now, does it, Dad?"

It went silent for a few seconds.

"Why don't you just come home, so we can talk about it, Dad? Lester is worried about you."

"Hmm!" he answered. Even the unobservant JP knew that Lester hadn't worried about anything since his dummy fell out of the pram when he was a year old.

"How's your doctor friend, Liza?"

"We're taking it slowly."

"No wedding bells then?"

"Dad!"

"Well, I'll need to save up some money if you're getting married."

"Look, Dad."

JP sensed she was about to harangue him again about returning home.

"How about I give you a call tomorrow, darling?"

"Just tell me where you are then?"

"Yes, I'll ring you tomorrow. Love to Robert. Oh, and Lester."

Even before JP married, his son Lester Preparé was always going to be named after his grandfather John, Preparé. Indeed his father was named John, and this had been the preferred first name, dating back to their French heritage when, of course, it was Jean. Indeed, the John had always been spelt as Jean and accompanied by a hyphenated second Christian name. JP refused to refer to a first name. In truth, the hyphenated names were necessary to avoid confusion. Anyone who has read Dickens *A Tale of Two Cities* will be all too familiar with the disorder caused by too many Jacques. So descendants were either Jean-Claude or Jean-Pierre.

The fact that JP Preparé felt the need to name his first male child Jean even before his marriage took place came as no surprise to those who knew the family. The family motto was *'Make ready in advance'*, presumably in keeping with the meaning of the surname itself. This pre-requisite of marriage caused great disappointment to Rhonda, who loathed her father-in-law with a passion. It was he who always insisted on the use of the acute accent, or l'accent aigu, as he called it.

"No, no," he would say. "l'accent aigu must always be retained, for it removes any ambiguity of how the name Preparé should be pronounced."

"But it makes it difficult for the children at school," Rhonda objected. "There isn't even a l'accent aigu on a computer keyboard."

Rhonda conspired in many ways to change her fiancé's mind about the name of their first male child. Yet it seemed to no avail. Then, two weeks before their wedding in June 1977, JP drew a horse in the East Sussex Education Authority's Derby sweepstake. He had only bought a ticket through peer pressure in the staff room. The message he received from Head Office declared that he would receive the horse's name the next day. The first prize was £500.

"Oh," remarked Rhonda, as if she had seen something shocking in the newspaper she was reading. Her husband looked up from his book. But, before he could question her, she answered him. "There's a horse in the Derby named Blushing Groom, and it's the favourite. Wouldn't it be a wonderful coincidence if you drew that horse? The race is just one week before our wedding."

Her husband agreed that it would be a remarkable coincidence, signalling another opportunity for Rhonda to change the name of their unborn child.

"And," she continued, "he is being ridden by a French jockey."

JP's attention was seized, and he closed his book.

"This is too much of a coincidence, John," his wife declared. "If you draw this horse and it wins the Derby, then we must name our first child after the jockey." Her husband hesitated. "It's a message from the Gods, John. It would pay for our wedding. Venus is looking kindly upon us."

JP had not heard his wife in such lyrical tones before. However, his concern was muted by the facts. He had a £1 sweepstake ticket that could be worth £500. The odds must be 10,000-1. And, in any case, he hadn't even drawn this particular horse yet. The Gods might be in favour, but the odds certainly were not. He agreed, and Rhonda threw her arms around his neck.

"What's the jockey's name?" she asked.

"Henri Samani."

"Henri," he replied. His great-grandfather was Jean-Henri Preparé.

The following day, JP puffed a sigh of relief. He had not drawn Blushing Groom in the Derby, which was a disappointment in some respects because it was the favourite to win the race. No, he had not drawn a French horse but an Irish one. The Minstrel was being ridden by Lester Piggott.

"At least we won't have to name our first son Henri," sighed JP.

"No, but I quite like the name, Lester. It's unusual, different." Perhaps not as different as Jean-Henri, she thought to herself.

The fact that the suggestion to name their unborn son after a jockey still had a heartbeat came as a surprise to JP. But the coincidence was based on the name of the horse. Blushing Groom, he insisted. Rhonda hadn't finished the sentence. "It's not common." She didn't say 'like John,' but the words still wounded him.

"Lester?" He gasped

She smiled. He winced.

It was a nebulous argument, he convinced himself. Blushing Groom was the favourite. The French horse had destroyed all opposition in his previous races.

Retaining a contrary outlook, Rhonda told herself the same, albeit with a reassurance that the previous races had been in France. This was The Derby. This was Lester Piggott.

Rhonda wasn't especially endeared towards naming her child Lester. She simply saw it as a victory over her fiancé's uncompromising position. Indeed, Henri would only have been a partial reprieve. Henri-Jean was as bad as Jean-Henri.

JP took succour in knowing that The Minstrel would need to win The Derby, and his wife would still need to remember the agreement if and when they had a son. Little did he know that his consent would be written in a secret diary, recorded for posterity, by his determined wife.

The Minstrel won, Rhonda won, and a line of Jean's dating back to the Norman invasion was in jeopardy. In fact, the Preparé family came to England in the sixteenth century, fleeing an intolerant French king. Louis XV burned Huguenots at the stake or forced them to flee the country, as a young Lester told the family after finishing his history homework one evening. He was right. The Preparé family had nothing to thank the

French for, so Lester's grandfather's pride in being French was entirely misplaced.

Rhonda's small victory was to set the pattern for such future successes. She won against the odds, a bit like The Minstrel. And she often won after that, although for JP, it rarely felt like defeat. He loved her with an intensity and passion that never diminished, even when she left him. In fact, the sudden realisation of how much he loved her had been overwhelming when she left. In her absence, his love for her only grew deeper.

These early days of the marriage were difficult times for JP, who found himself taking comfort in hateful outcomes, each of which prevented the need to break the news to his father. He pondered on the ambiguity of the word conceivably. Maybe he wouldn't have a son. Perhaps his father would die before the birth of his son. Then again, his father might be on his deathbed, and the naming of his first grandson might be his dying wish. Conceivably, in such circumstances, Rhonda might change her mind. Conceivably she wouldn't conceive.

Rhonda did conceive, almost as quickly as The Minstrel won the Derby. The Sweepstake prize paid for the wedding, and the money they had saved for the wedding became a deposit on a house. The modest savings they had accumulated for their first house made only the tiniest impression on the cost of raising a child.

Distraught at the idea of having his first grandson named Lester, Grandfather considered disowning the child and separating his son from his inheritance for dishonouring the family tradition. And yet, who among us can resist the innocent charm of a baby? The resentment and malice dissolved the moment the tiny infant was placed in his arms. The more positive aspect of the situation, at least for the old man, was that Lester's name is spelt the same in French as English. So, who would know? And yet, the irony in the choice of name was that the word 'lester' meant 'ballast' in French. And the boy did, in fact, provide the ballast necessary in the tempestuous relationship between JP and his father.

As he unpacked his suitcase at the hotel, those difficult yet treasured memories triggered a distant recollection of the diaries that Rhonda kept in those early years. They had long been disposed of. JP searched for them, of course, when she left, but to no avail. His last recollection of a diary was 2014, coincidently when they stayed at the San Giovanni Resort, here in Saluzzo. It was the hotel that had triggered his thoughts on the subject. He wondered why Rhonda had stopped keeping a diary. Was this around the time she told him about the affair?

For several years, JP had taken to arranging their annual holidays himself online. But the remoteness of some parts of Italy meant it was only possible to see them by hiring a car, which JP had no intention of doing. When they decided to visit the Piedmonte area, JP, against his better judgement, was forced to use the services of a travel company. The twin-centre holiday included five days in Turin and another five relaxing in Saluzzo. The whole concept of a package holiday railed against his dislike of strangers. JP snubbed the organised elements of the trip. His long periods of reticence were overpowered only by his ungovernable urge to contradict the official guide.

"It's Romanesque," JP pointed out to the guide as they were taken around Susa Cathedral. The inevitable comment came much to the annoyance of Rhonda. "Gothic architecture has pointed arches," JP pointed out, "whilst Romanesque has semi-circular ones."

The owners of the San Giovanni Hotel refer to it as a resort. Eight years ago, the former monastery provided a relaxing atmosphere after JP and Rhonda conducted some energetic sightseeing around Turin. The fifteenth-century building has an old refectory, presumably used for weddings, though JP had never seen one there. And there is a beautiful cloister where he and Rhonda had enjoyed a memorable lunch. Predictably, JP had deliberately avoided the other group members at all times except where necessary to take in the sights. This evening would be different. Tonight he would dine alone in the unusual barrel-shaped vault of the hotel's restaurant.

With the photograph of his wife in his jacket pocket, JP went downstairs for a drink. In the bar, the waiter offered a smile and a glimmer of recognition. It was a good start, but JP wanted a gin and tonic and for the waiter to say he'd seen Rhonda earlier that day. Then the journey would be over, and he wouldn't have to speak to strangers like the barman. Although the glimpses of recognition suggested, he wasn't a complete stranger. For the moment, the photo remained concealed in his pocket, and JP began with some small talk, an attempt at creating a back story that didn't slander his wife.

In a cocktail of English and Italian, he asked if any historical sites in the surrounding area were near enough to visit by taxi.

The waiter responded in Italian. "Ma sei stato qui prima." He realised JP did not completely understand him. "But you have been here before, I believe."

The clarification in English did not deter JP from pushing on with some stilted Italian. "Era un pacchetto vacanza. Siamo andati dove siamo stati portati." JP's pronunciation was poor. He could see that on the man's face. So he reluctantly threw some light on the statement. "My wife and I were on a package holiday. We went where we were taken."

The man wiped some glasses with a cloth but made no comment on the absence of JP's wife. "There is little to see in Saluzzo itself," he answered, ignoring JP's attempt at Italian. "However, the surrounding area is a treasure trove of medieval castles and baroque buildings."

As JP remembered it, the advice was correct. Even though much of the fifteenth-century walled town was intact, there wasn't much to see in Saluzzo itself. The place's charm was its hilltop setting, its picturesque squares, charming cobbled streets and elegant palazzos.

The waiter recommended the Castle and the Basilica in the Piazza Risorgimento.

"Yes, I will visit the Basilica of the Assumption," JP replied, placing emphasis on the word I.

The waiter's expression did not change. He had no intention about enquiring after the man's wife. Discretion is a prerequisite of the barman's job.

When they visited here eight years ago, JP and Rhonda had walked the Ascent to the Castle, as the locals called it. And Rhonda admired the frescoes and terracotta decorations along the way. He recalled standing at the Casa Cavassa, admiring the panoramic views of Monte Viso. And JP took a photograph of Rhonda standing in Griselda Street, dedicated to a character in the final tale from Boccaccio's *Decameron*. He framed it for Liza when they got home. The story of Griselda was a strange one, politically incorrect, as are many of Boccaccio's ancient folk stories. It praised a wife's obedience and submission. JP sipped his gin and tonic and smiled at how times had changed.

"My wife particularly liked Susa Cathedral," replied JP returning to his natural tongue. "But it will be easier to reach when I move on to Turin in two days."

The barman agreed, and, as JP removed the photograph from his pocket, he noticed the lapel badge on the man's waistcoat.

"This is my wife, Gennaro."

"She is beautiful," the barman replied, trying to be as polite as possible.

"We're meeting up on the trip," JP explained. "I work abroad," he lied, "so we travelled here from different places." There was hesitance in his words and a sense of improvisation. "My wife couldn't be certain where she could join me. For all I know, she may already be here. I forgot to ask at reception." JP was conscious that his explanation was protracted and rambling. "Have you seen her around recently?"

"L'hai vista di recente?" JP asked, not fully understanding why he chose to repeat the question in Italian when the barman spoke perfectly good English.

"She looks familiar," Gennaro answered encouragingly.

"We were here eight years ago."

The barman nodded knowingly.

"Have you?" JP stammered, hesitating to finish the question. Gennaro thought he might be about to ask for olives or nuts. But JP was now waving the photograph in front of his face.

"Have you seen her?"

"No, not recently," he answered, stepping backwards to avoid the breeze from the flapping photograph.

JP grasped at the word recently. He couldn't remember how long Rhonda had been missing. "This year?" he asked.

"No."

The young man sounded a little annoyed at the cross-examination, so JP rather clumsily switched the conversation back to the local sights. "What about the amphitheatre at Ivrea and the aqueduct at Acqui Terme?"

"The same can be said of these places," Gennaro told him. "They are easier to reach from Turin than from Saluzzo.

The waiter was relieved when a younger couple walked into the bar and ordered some drinks. JP's enquiries had revealed nothing, so he sat at a table and checked his watch.

JP was indeed keen to visit at least one of the tourist spots the waiter mentioned. On their previous visit, he and Rhonda had made the booking with a travel agent, and the coach excursions were part of the reservation. He didn't expect to find his wife at any of these places anyway. It would be a pure coincidence if JP happened to stumble upon her on the exact day they both decided to visit some obscure monument in Piedmonte. And yet, wasn't the basis of the whole trip that he might stumble upon her, just as he had done so in sixth form college? A voice in his head assured him that lightning doesn't strike the same place twice. "Nonsense," JP answered, attracting the attention of the couple at the bar. 'Lightning propagation is almost commonplace,' he silently rebuked the misinformed notion. 'There is evidence of lightning striking the same place twice in Texas and Mexico.' The couple standing at the bar tried not to stare at the strange man whose lips were moving silently. JP got up and went into the restaurant for dinner.

When her father failed to call her the following day, Liza took herself off to the old family home. Her weekly visits to her parents' house were rarely on the same day but conducted randomly in the hope of catching her father at home. On this occasion, this dutiful daughter was less surprised to find her father absent than on previous visits. JP's daily walk had become a twice-daily exercise. Sometimes increasing to three outings when he had forgotten one of the other two. And, on one occasion, he actually went out four times, having buried two previous strolls under an accumulation of ideas and plans. The timing of his walks was less predictable than his daughter's trips home, which resulted in her not seeing him on most visits. She disliked sitting in the house alone, so she made herself busy, tidying up, dead-heading some plants, and occasionally leaving some food. More recently, she took to clearing out some of her mother's clothes or shoes. Today was different, however. Today there was a purpose to her visit.

For one thing, she didn't expect to find her father at home. The unnerving phone call she received suggested he was out of the country. However, she did not believe his excuse of buying duty-free wine. And, if he wasn't buying wine, then there was little reason to believe the rest of his fanciful tale. The only verifiable evidence was the foreign ring tone. Liza suddenly had an idea and rushed to check the garage. She found the car parked there and cursed herself for not bothering to look when she popped round last week. There had been no point because she assumed her father was out walking. Liza missed several clues on that visit. She didn't go upstairs; otherwise, her father's absence would have been apparent. She couldn't be sure that he'd left by then, but she wouldn't have noticed if that had been the case. Her whirlwind visit had been delayed and rushed. Trapped between a Zoom meeting and a dinner date with Robert. So her father could have been gone for eight days, but the bins had been emptied and put back in place, so he must have left after Thursday. The certainty that she had spoken to him on Thursday made the evidence confusing.

Upstairs some guide books and maps suggested her father might be in Italy rather than Calais. Liza believed she understood her father's motives for the trip. But she couldn't make sense of his furtive behaviour. If he planned to take some time away, then Liza would happily have joined him. She examined the evidence, but her father didn't damage maps or books by scribbling on them. Any plans would be in a journal.

As she stood looking out the bedroom window at the garden below, she stabbed at her mobile phone.

"Lester?"

A recognisable moan followed as her brother retrieved his mobile phone from its burial ground on the sofa.

"Lester, Daddy's gone somewhere. Well, Italy, probably, or perhaps France."

"Oh, that's nice."

"It's not nice, and he's not answering his phone. I spoke to him on Thursday – at least, I believe it was Thursday, and the ring tone suggested he was abroad. He said he was in Calais."

"I thought you said he wasn't answering his phone."

"He's stopped taking my calls. He says he drove to Calais, but the car is still in the garage. I'm round his place now, and there are maps and tourist guides on his desk."

"That's nice. The break will do him good."

"Stop saying 'that's nice', Lester, it's not nice, it's very worrying. You should be worried too. I can't be expected to...." She stopped mid-sentence. "We need to get into his computer to find out where he has gone. According to this map, he could be anywhere in Italy or southern France."

"I can think of worse places to be right now."

"We need to find the password to Dad's computer. He would have planned the whole trip online, travel, hotel, the lot. He plans everything. He's not playing this by ear."

"Most older people have passwords connected to their kids. Try *Give us a Clue*. Mum and Dad liked that programme. Always talking about it. You do know you're named after Liza Goddard, don't you? She was a panel member."

His sister ignored the last remark.

"Actually, I heard you were going to be Alvin if you had been a boy," he continued. "Named after Alvin Stardust. Must have been something to do with him marrying Liza Goddard, I reckon."

The story Lester had heard was true, of course. Alvin was the most outrageous suggestion Rhonda could come up with at the time. JP used so much of his energy opposing the name that he completely lost sight of his own proposal. His suggestion of Jean-Louis was defeated on the first ballot. Of course, when Rhonda became pregnant the second time, there was a prolonged debate on what their next son should be named. This was followed by a rush to name a baby girl that nobody was expecting.

"Amongst the discarded notes, maps and old photographs, there's an empty picture frame which I'm sure contained a photo of Mum. The wardrobe and drawers suggest he has packed a case and left."

"Look, Liza, Dad has simply taken himself off for a few days to get his head together. Sounds like a good idea to me."

"Then why is he not taking my calls."

"Because he knows you're a worrier, and the last thing he needs right now is someone crowding him. Give him some space. He'll be home in a few days."

"Do you know what his password is?" The impatience in her voice was growing.

"No, I don't. But it will be something to do with Mum or you. Or perhaps me, but probably not. Or, it could be Henri Fayol. He was always banging on about him."

"Henri Fayol?" she asked before spelling it.

"Yes, or I suppose you could try Rhonda Watson. Not a particularly difficult to crack, though, it being mum's maiden name."

"Is that the best you can do? You did a degree in Computer Science, didn't you?"

"I dropped out, Liza. You do remember that don't you?"

She did remember the episode and how annoyed her father was. He'd warned Lester that Computer Science was the subject with the highest drop-out rate. There's a whole world of youngsters wanting to be game designers or cybersecurity agents. But it's just not like that, he warned his wayward son.

"Well, don't you remember anything of the first year?" Liza urged. "I just need to get into Dad's computer."

"I'm not sure the first thing on the syllabus would be how to break into someone else's computer."

"Perhaps you should finish the course," she suggested. "There's plenty of vacancies out there for web developers."

"It pays £20,000 a year, Sis. I can earn more than that with temporary work for Royal Mail leading up to Christmas."

"You could earn a lot more if you put in the overtime they offered you."

"If people work overtime, they deny some other poor bastard a job. Royal Mail should be in public ownership and bring an end to exploitation and this dictatorship of the proletariat."

"Your socialist views just show you how much a red-brick education can damage your view of life."

"I was only at Reading University for one year. I wasn't there long enough to cause any damage."

"It was enough to get you a job with that smart tech company in Surrey."

"A bunch of private-educated bastards. Anti-working class, anti-Gingers. Do you know, they referred to me as Simply Redbrick?"

"That's very cruel."

"Oh, it didn't touch what I called them when we had the argument."

"What argument?"

"The one just before they sacked me."

"Another spell of unemployment was there?"
"I've never been unemployed."
"Yes, you have."
"I've been out of work, but Dad insisted I never signed on. He couldn't stand the shame."
"What he funded you while you were lazing about?"
"Look," Lester interrupted. "You can't draw a pension until you're sixty-eight years old now. And yet, the qualifying period for a full state pension is thirty-five years. That means I can rest for twelve years in my working life and still qualify for a full pension. I don't make the rules, Sis."

Liza ignored her brother's self-pitying political rant and renewed her appeal. "If you have any ideas on how to get into Dad's computer, will you please call me? Just apply yourself to the problem for a few minutes."

That evening, Liza left two voicemails for her father, a WhatsApp message, and a lengthy text. A photo of the empty picture frame was attached to the WhatsApp message, which told her father she knew where he was. Liza regretted the wording when she read through her efforts later. She didn't know where he was. That was the problem. But she had a good idea he was somewhere in Italy trying to recover from the ordeal of the last few months. The following morning she received a reply on WhatsApp, with a photograph of a statue attached. It was a man standing on a plinth surrounded by a wrought iron fence.

'This is a monument of the Italian poet Silvio Pellico. I'm not sure if you're familiar with him. I'm not

really in Calais. I'm in Italy. Your mum has gone, and I can't sit at home doing nothing. I'm quite alright, so don't worry.'

Liza hadn't heard of Pellico, so she looked him up on the internet. His best work was written in prison, it seems, and his Canzone spoke of the lone captive's sinking heart wrapped in a living tomb. More importantly, the statue was in the Italian town of Saluzzo. She remembered her parents visiting there about eight or ten years ago.

Liza forwarded the message to her brother, suggesting they meet at the family home to access their father's computer. That way, they could find out where he was heading next. Lester was a bit of a geek when it came to computers, and Liza hoped he would find a way of accessing their dad's one. Lester didn't reply.

"Well, he's in Saluzzo by the sound of it," Lester told her when she phoned him ten minutes later.

"No, I called the hotel, and he checked out this morning. They didn't know if he was going home or simply travelling somewhere else."

"When the time comes, elderly people lose their marbles very quickly," her brother commented sagely.

"Hmm! You're not helping Lester. Dad's been away for days now. Anything could have happened."

"And, has anything happened?"

"Not that I know of."

"Well, so far, so good, then."

"That could be your motto, Lester. So far, so good."

"How did you know which hotel he was staying in?"

"Because I pay attention, Lester. I listen when people talk to me. And I remembered that's where Mum and Dad stayed when they visited there about ten years ago."

"Well, he's probably on his way home now."

"Hmm! He's not on his way home, Lester. I know it sounds weird, but I'm worried he might be looking for mum."

The comment made her brother laugh.

She tried to ignore his chuckling. "What are you laughing at, Lester? It happens."

"I thought you were talking metaphorically."

"Metaphysically, more like."

"Don't go all Gothic on me, Liza. I haven't been awake that long."

"I'm going back to the house, and I'm going to get into Dad's computer. He plans his holidays with military precision. Every detail of his trip will be on that computer, including the hotels. If you have any bright ideas about what the password might be, then let me know."

Nothing is just the way it is. Things happen for a reason because every action has a reaction. The logic of the argument wasn't lost on JP, who was trying to arrange a taxi to take him to Turin. Each action has a cause, a trigger. Rhonda left for a reason. Why was he taking a cab when a bus would be much cheaper? The cause and effect behind this decision were much easier to fathom than his wife's reasons for leaving him.

Unlike many events of the past few months, the bus ride from Cuneo was still fresh in JP's memory. Although fresh is not a word he would readily associate with the journey. Having been tortured by the number ninety bus, volunteering for further punishment by travelling to Turin by a number ninety-one bus was simply inviting trouble. Was redemption from an hour of torture worth around one hundred euros? He decided it was.

The taxi ride from Saluzzo to Turin needed to be pre-booked, and the price was based on several component parts. The route, the journey time, and the time of day or night had to be computed, together with any changes to the fare rate when entering the city. The best estimate the hotel could give JP was that it would cost ninety euros, ten times the cost of travelling by Linea 091 bus. But it would be considerably less unpleasant than repeating his experience of a few days ago.

"Has the taxi got air-conditioning?" JP asked the hotel receptionist as he checked out that morning. A quizzical face looked back at him. "Ha l'auto ha l'aria condizionata?" JP repeated in Italian.

She nodded. "Certamente, naturalmente." Her hand gestures supported the authoritativeness of the statement.

Such brash statements from Italians filled JP with scepticism. 'Certainly, naturally,' had little more value in Italian than the words perhaps, maybe or possibly in English. He recalled an Irishman he knew, long ago, who ended most sentences with the words 'God willing.' It was an expression easily translated into Italian.

Ten minutes later, the taxi rattled away from the dry hotel car park, and dust flew through the driver's window before dissolving in the damp heat of the car. God willing, or otherwise, the windows were the only form of air conditioning in operation.

"Ha l'auto ha l'aria condizionata?" JP asked the driver.

"Si, certamente."

"Well, can you turn it on then?" He scrambled to see if he had his Italian phrasebook on him. He didn't, it was in his suitcase, so he tried to work out how to tell the driver to turn on the air conditioning.

"Su" was the best he could come up with. "On."

"Accenderlo?" asked the driver.

"Si, si, accenderlo per favore."

Suddenly JP had a change of heart and a change of mind. This section of the plan could be completed in two parts, which would serve two purposes. Firstly it would break this monotonous journey, and secondly, it would enable him to take in another location and provide an opportunity to find Rhonda.

"Fermarta!" he called above the roaring sound of the air conditioning. "Cambio!"

The taxi pulled to a sudden halt, and the driver asked his passenger if he had no money. Not money, not change as in cash, he thought to himself, chastising his poor language skills. Not money – change the destination. "Modificare la destinazione."

"Ah, si," the man replied. "Torino, non Turin."

"No, no," declared JP, switching to English to ensure he gave the correct instructions. "I don't want to go to Turin. Non Torino!" He shuffled around, looking for his phrasebook. "Puoi portarmi all'ampiteatro per favore," he said. "I want to go to the amphitheatre. Ampiteatro di Ivrea."

"Ivrea," the driver confirmed.

"Si, Ivrea. Il amphitheatre."

"Anfiteatro Romano di Ivrea," he replied.

"Si," answered JP.

The driver shrugged and set off towards the new destination.

JP had all day to make the relatively short journey to Turin. It wasn't some strange ethereal message that sent him to Ivrea, just a fragile hope that Rhonda might be there. It took almost the same amount of time to reach Ivrea as it would have to get to Turin, but JP felt he was making better use of the day. When the taxi dropped him off, JP looked around the deserted car park and followed the signs, pulling his suitcase behind him.

Under a scorching midday sun, JP sat in the amphitheatre, wondering how his beloved absent companion might console the trials of the day. It felt comfortable that Rhonda must be gazing at this very sky. She's just sitting somewhere else, he told himself. He regretted sharing the business of her affair, telling people about her momentary lapse, embarrassing her in front of strangers. Their relationship was unique, their loves equal in all respects. Turning the events of the trip in his mind, he languished in semi-dejection, recalling that juvenile betrayal of his wife. A heart that had once broken faith should not be condemned forever. It was a mistake, and her leaving had no connection to that brief lapse on her part. He was sure of that.

The stopover at Ivrea had been just another distraction, and it added nothing to the mission other than to tick a box. So he resolved to go to another place, to move on to Turin to find her.

The amphitheatre wasn't a popular tourist spot. It was as old as the Colosseum in Rome but consisted of little more than the foundations. As he walked back to the car park, he realised he didn't have a number for a taxi and would probably have to wait until one turned up to drop someone off. He sat wondering why Liza wanted the password to his computer. Of course, he knew the answer, but he just hoped there could be some innocent reason that had nothing to do with her turning up at the next place on the itinerary. JP thought about changing the plan, an almost inconceivable idea. He had changed the program to visit Ivrea, and this move hadn't proved very successful. So he convinced himself to let the plan run its course. There were several promising places to visit along the journey to Bellagio.

Strangely, it was the password to his computer that had triggered thoughts about the naming of Lester. He sat musing on past holidays in the amphitheatre of Ivrea with a mixture of fond and thorny memories. One of the thorniest was a day trip to Susa Cathedral when Rhonda had her toe bitten by a small dog. They had been trying to find a free table at an outdoor café, winding their way through the crowd hoping to enjoy a glass of wine out of the hot sunshine. Suddenly a tiny Pekinese dog locked its teeth on Rhonda's toe. A scene from another Italian opera followed as JP wrenched at the dog's lead, only making the situation worse. Eventually, it let go, and after a debate with the owners, a waiter and the café owner, JP was forced to take his wife to the local hospital for a tetanus injection. It should have presented an excellent opportunity for JP to practice his Italian language skills. After all, he had time to construct the sentence in his head.

Fully prepared, JP rushed his wife to the reception and declared: "Un piccolo cane e mangiata mia moglie."

The receptionist looked at JP and the woman standing next to him. Then called for someone who could speak English. A young nurse arrived to ask what the problem was.

"Un piccolo cane ha mangiato la moglie di quest'uomo," her colleague told her.

The nurse laughed and then stifled the sound by clasping her mouth with her hand. She recovered herself. "A small dog has eaten your wife?" she asked.

"Bitten my wife," an embarrassed JP corrected himself. "On the toe. Someone suggested she might need a tetanus injection."

The incident ended well. They had to pay for the injection before it would be administered. But they were soon in a taxi on their way back to the hotel after missing their trip to the amphitheatre.

Maybe she would come back here, thought JP as he sat in the hot sun. Return here, like he had done so, to recover that lost day. Or perhaps to remember it.

Of all the provinces of Italy, Rhonda loved Piedmonte. Even though Bellagio was in Lombardy and the abiding memory of Piedmonte would always be the trip to the hospital. So, for their last holiday together before the pandemic began, JP produced an innovative itinerary. Not that he knew the pandemic was coming. He planned something special for their holiday every year. In fact, each year had to outdo the previous one. Each new adventure must be something that will take her breath away. This new adventure would begin in Antibes, just to throw her off the scent. Then a scenic train journey from the South of France to that small town in the southern part of Piedmonte named Cuneo, which they visited five years before.

And so, three years later, he decided to start the search to find her where that last holiday in Antibes began. He would return to the place where they last travelled together before she ran away. It was as good a place as any to start, but he knew the search would move to Italy, beginning with Piedmonte, to the towns they visited eight years ago. It was to be a holiday to take her breath away. Instead, it took her away.

"It was eight years ago, not ten," JP corrected his daughter when she called him again. "We came here eight years ago. Your mum was bitten by a small dog."

Liza was pleased he remembered both the year of that holiday with mum and the episode of the dog. "Yes, you told me that story, Dad." Then, without hesitation, she added: "You didn't text me the password."

The uninterrupted transition from one subject to another took JP by surprise. No, he hadn't texted her the password, and he didn't intend to if he could avoid it. He needed to change the subject. Otherwise, this mission would turn into something else.

"There isn't anyone else," JP told Liza reluctantly, wondering if his daughter knew about her mother's affair.

The slightly cryptic message was misunderstood by his daughter. "I know that, Dad. Everyone knows that Mum's the only one for you."

"No, I don't mean me," he answered. "Of course, there is no one else for me. I meant there wasn't anyone else for your mother."

"No, Dad, of course there never was anyone else for Mum," she answered.

JP's thoughts were divided. Was she lying out of kindness to her vulnerable father, or was she really unaware of her mother's infidelity? Mothers share everything with their daughters, don't they?

"Your mother had an affair, Liza." He was relieved to have spoken the words.

"She didn't have an affair, Dad. She would have told me. She told me everything."

JP thought about it and accepted that this statement was probably true. Rhonda might not tell him everything, but she probably told Liza.

"Where are you, Dad?"

"Actually, I'm not far from where your mother was bitten by the dog. I'm at the amphitheatre we were supposed to visit that day."

"Where are you staying?" She didn't tell him she had already spoken with the hotel at Saluzzo.

"I'm waiting for a taxi to take me to Turin."

"To do what?"

"Oh, just doing some sightseeing," he lied.

Liza was pleased to hear that her father had no ulterior motive for his actions, even though she suspected the opposite was true.

"When are you coming home?"

"Soon," he answered.

"How long will you be in Turin?"

"No more than two nights."

"And then home?"

"Let's see."

JP thought on this conversation as he sat waiting for a taxi to pull into the car park. He had no idea when that might occur, but he wasn't particularly looking forward to the sterile business hotel in Turin, anyway. He'd considered other hotels in the city, but this was the one he had stayed in with Rhonda. He knew she wouldn't be there, but it was a good stopping off point.

Cars came and went, and JP asked a few drivers if they were taxi drivers. It wasn't always obvious, and he didn't want to miss an opportunity to leave the dusty car park. As he sat thinking, something bothered him. Why would Rhonda not tell her daughter about the affair? After all, she eventually told him. JP's logical mind set about the problem is like a mathematical puzzle. He soon concluded that there could be only one reason.

JP was familiar with the devices Rhonda used to get her own way. Not that they were ever predictable. The naming of Lester was only the first of her many contrived and convoluted victories. Choosing to take flight to get her own way was not unexpected. However, on this occasion, JP couldn't actually recall what she wanted to get her own way about. They had been discussing holidays, but she always left that to him. Perhaps that was it. She had finally grown tired of JP always deciding where they went on holiday. Obviously, his planning those holidays with military precision wearied her. Owing to Covid, there had been two years since their last holiday, so perhaps she just wanted a change. JP couldn't think of any other reason for her to desert him. There was the affair, of course, but that was in the distant past. And JP was convinced that Rhonda had moved on from that incident. The times had changed, and they were different people now. But Rhonda had chosen not to tell her daughter about the affair, and there must have been a very good reason for that.

Eventually, a taxi pulled up to drop off a couple of tourists. The driver said the journey would take less than one hour, and he was familiar with the hotel that JP was staying in. The young man was pleased to find a fare in such a remote location. He spoke a little English, and JP was too tired to try speaking Italian.

"The cost is ninety."

"Euros?" JP asked stupidly. What else could it be? The days of the lira are long past.

JP passed the rather tedious journey converting the taxi fare from euros to sterling and then into lira. With a tip that would be 220,000 lire, he smiled to himself. Lira was of a romantic age. It carried fond memories of those early days in Italy. Those days of cash and travellers' cheques, instead of credit cards and Revolut. JP was at work then, so Rhonda had to obtain the traveller's cheques from the bank. And it was she who needed to sign them when converting them to cash during the holiday. The taxi journey continued with pleasant thoughts of lunch on the lakeside at Garda, back in those early days of holidays without kids in tow. Lavarello, the local fish, with salad cost 10,000 lire, the message read on the small blackboard outside the covered terrace. Cash, of course. JP recalled that, more recently, the Italian Government introduced a new law to prevent money laundering. This dictated that all bills over 1,000 euros could not be paid in cash. He visited a restaurant and joked that such a law could not have worked with lira.

"Laws change nothing," the owner told him confidently, adding that he preferred cash.

"Not possible for bills over 1,000 euros," JP commented.

"All things are possible."

"What if my bill was more than 1,000 euros and I wanted to pay in cash?" JP taunted.

"Then I would simply give you two bills," came the cynical reply.

Holidays for the Preparé family began in Hastings when Lester was a baby. Those holidays inspired their love for the area, which prompted them to move from London a few years later. Holidays in the UK continued until the summer Lester was to move to secondary school. This and the new decade prompted the family to take their first holiday abroad. However, the decision was JP's, who, somewhat selfishly, took them to Bellagio. It was the archetypal Italian lakeside village but not the perfect venue for children. And yet, despite the lack of theme parks, playgrounds and beaches, it was an enchanting world for all of them. As the aircraft stood on the runway at Gatwick Airport, JP told his children he had some fairy dust in his pocket to make sure they were taken to a new wonderful land of adventure. There was very little adventure but breathtaking views of places they had only imagined.

Lesson learned, holidays through the nineties were chosen with the kids in mind. Taormina, Menorca, Majorca and the Spanish mainland. Rhonda and JP didn't enjoy a holiday without the children until Liza went to university to study European Literature, the subject she had learned to love through those very same holidays. That first holiday abroad without their children was a short break to Rome.

Her father had introduced Liza to Italian literature during their annual holidays there in the nineties. Similar cultural breaks to Florence and Bologna were followed by twin-centre holidays to places like Rome and Sorrento or Venice and Lake Garda. There were intermittent visits to Austria, Cyprus and Turkey, but once the kids had flown the nest, it was always Italy

Twenty years had passed since the Euro replaced the Lira. It was the year of JP and Rhonda's silver wedding anniversary, twelve years after their first visit to Bellagio. The year before those final days of the old currency, they spent a week in Bologna, when the exchange rate was 2,500 lira to £1 sterling. But it was the holidays on Italy's lakes that brought the fondest memories of those almost worthless notes when a 1,000 lira note was worth forty pence. It was how JP remembered the constantly steady exchange rate. £4 for a lunch of Lavarello and salad. JP forgot how much wine cost back then. But it was a carafe rather than a bottle. A carafe of Custoza, JP thought to himself. It was these cherished memories that fuelled his journey. As the taxi approached the city of Turin, JP recalled those friends who had been lost along the way, like carafes, lira, dessert trolleys in restaurants, traveller's cheques and Rhonda, of course.

6

Turin, Piedmonte

Meeting people for the first time was not a situation that JP relished nor, indeed, had ever mastered. He always made a cumbersome entrance and often an awkward bow when he left. Speaking in Italian helped in some strange way. It broke the ice each time he was forced to talk to someone new on holiday. It wasn't always successful, of course. He once ordered a bottle of Custoza and received a bottle of lemonade. It was only when he asked where his wine was that he realised the Italian word for lemonade was gassosa.

The challenge of being a misoxenist abroad was mitigated only by dogmatism on JP's part. He didn't feel able or obliged to correct people's grammar, a characteristic which made him seem pedantry at home. Nor was he able to express excessive displays of self-knowledge, which made him look conceited. However, he was still precise in everything he did.

The distinguished-looking gentleman working on the reception desk of the Turin Palace Hotel did not recognise JP, even when he asked him to reserve a table at Ristorante Del Cambio that evening. JP was distracted by Déjà Vu, as he recalled doing the same thing on his last visit to the hotel, except tonight it would be a table for one.

"Do you require assistance with your luggage, sir?" The question brought him back to the present.

"No," replied JP, removing the photograph of Rhonda from his jacket pocket. "I'm meeting my wife here. Has she checked in yet?"

The clerk ignored the photograph and looked at his computer screen, mumbling "Preparé," in three distinct syllables.

JP thrust the photograph in front of the man's face. "She may be using another name." The clerk had heard similar unlikely stories before, so he was not surprised as JP fumbled for a suitable explanation. "She's a famous author."

The young man examined the photograph and shrugged his shoulders. The woman didn't look like a prostitute, but each to his own. He looked again at the computer screen.

"And she writes under what name?" he asked a little cynically.

"Sorry," explained JP as he tried to find a way out of the corner he had painted himself into. "You speak perfect English." It was a blunt trauma compliment.

113

"Thank you, sir. The name?"

"It doesn't matter. My wife uses many."

"Many?"

"She ghost-writes for several people. Have you seen her?" The photo was waved again.

"No, sir. I'm sorry, I have not seen your wife. Do you have separate rooms?"

"We're travelling separately. My wife wasn't sure she could make it."

It was 2014 when they last visited Turin together. One week in Saluzzo and another in Turin, with organised coach trips to the many sites in the area. Scotland had voted to remain part of the UK, and Crimea was annexed by Russia. The people of Hong Kong were protesting about being part of China, and Ukraine didn't want to be part of Russia. The world seemed to be consumed by the cementing and fragmenting of relationships. JP wasn't sure why all this seemed relevant, but they happened when he and Rhonda were last in Turin. This time it was a relationship of a more personal nature that was fragmenting.

"Have you tried phoning your wife, sir?" There was a growing tone of sarcasm in the man's voice.

"Non importa," declared JP. He thanked the clerk and headed off to the lift.

JP was getting quicker at unpacking. He examined some shirts and found a laundry bag in the wardrobe. Time for some cleaning, he thought as he took his toiletries into the bathroom. Splashing some water on his face, he began another rehearsal. Could the long-awaited meeting be conducted without questions or interrogation? Yes, he convinced himself, with a simple confession, that life was impossible without her. No questions, he mumbled to himself. No irritable searching for cause or reason. And then he was left with just two words. "Come home," he told the mirror. The intonation was too dictatorial. "Come home," he repeated only this time with an imploring inflexion in his voice.

There were only a few familiar places to be ticked off the list in Turin. The city stood at the foot of the Alps and was essentially an industrial centre now. It was the home to Fiat, Alessi, Kappa, Ferrero, Martini-Bacardi, and, of course, the famous football club, Juventus. But it had its history too. As any local will tell you, it was the first capital city of a unified Italy. And, it has many fine attractions, most of which JP ignored as he wandered around the city.

 Rhonda wasn't keen on the Egyptian Museum or the sixteenth century Royal Palace, a former residence of the Savoy dynasty. And she certainly wasn't interested in the car museum, which was entirely at home in Italy's own Motown. This just left three possibilities, the most popular of which was the Museum of the Shroud. There would be a long queue and only a faint chance of locating Rhonda there. He hoped, beyond hope, that one of these two places is where he might find her.

He strolled around the Parco del Valentino and its Medieval village. He then set off to the most promising of Turin's sights. The National Cinema Museum was a favourite venue of Rhonda's when they last visited here. An iconic building that was initially intended to be a synagogue until the money ran out. *From here to Eternity*, had exhibits, as did the Italian's favourite Burt Lancaster movie, *The Leopard*, which JP considered one of his best acting roles.

The café in the museum only sold panini, and after the tasteless panini on the train, he decided against it. Instead, he popped into a small Bistro, the Montebello, opposite the entrance to the museum.

There was no sign of Rhonda in the museum, and JP held out little hope of finding her in the bar. His disappointment was two-fold when he discovered how well the staff spoke English. But that same staff served excellent wine by the glass and some tasty tapas too. He looked about the small restaurant. With no sign of Rhonda and having booked a table for dinner, he chose a small salami and cheese board whilst wondering why food isn't served on plates anymore. Turin is the home of Vermouth, but JP opted for a glass of local Barolo red wine. He flicked through the museum brochure paying little attention to the movie poster of Casablanca with the archetypal picture of Humphrey Bogart. But, strangely, the famous scene from that iconic movie was about to be played out right in front of him. Across the room, a man was staring at him, squinting a little and wiping his spectacles as if he couldn't believe what he was looking at. He was looking at JP. The man hesitated, and, picking up his glass, he strode purposefully towards JP's table.

From a short distance away, he began talking. "It is you, isn't it?" JP tried to place him without success. He could confirm it was him, but who was asking the question?

"Ringo!" the man announced to anyone within fifty metres who wished to listen. A few people in the bar looked around, half expecting to see Ringo Starr. JP hadn't been called Ringo since his university days.

"Of all the bars in all the towns in all the world," the man added as he flopped into a chair on JP's table.

Humphrey Bogart stared back at JP as the almost familiar man stole his famous line.

JP was rummaging through his memory banks. Through the balding grey hair and thick-rimmed glasses, he saw a face that was almost recognisable from nearly fifty years ago. Names flashed before him as he rushed through the alphabet.

JP covered his thoughts with a grinning smile and arrived at Mark, Martin, Malcolm.

"Malcolm. Well, well, well. Malcolm Chandler. How are you?"

But, before the man could reply, JP intervened. "By the way, it's gin joints, not bars."

Malcolm looked bemused.

"Of all the gin joints, in all the towns, in all the world, that's the Bogart line in Casablanca."

"Right," replied Malcolm.

"Anyway, I interrupted you."

"Mustn't complain, old man, but then nobody listens when I do. You haven't changed."

"I must look much older," replied JP.

"No, I mean, you're still correcting people."

The comment went over JP's head. "Nineteen seventy-four," he declared. "Nobody's called me Ringo since nineteen seventy-four. In fact, you were the only person who did call me Ringo back then."

"Yes," replied Malcolm. "Well, with a name like John Paul, what would we call you but Ringo."

Sartre and Getty came to mind, but JP kept the thought to himself. "I'm not sure they would think of Ringo anymore." JP declared, sounding a little too indignant. "John Paul the Second became more famous than Ringo Starr, I imagine."

"They also called you the Jean Genie. Something to do with the David Bowie song."

JP couldn't remember that.

"Did I hear that you ended up marrying Rhoda?"

"Rhonda," JP corrected him. "Yes, nearly 45 years we've been married now."

Malcolm ignored the comment and moved the conversation swiftly away from marriage to football. "Are you here for the match too? I don't remember you being a Spurs fan."

The expression on JP's face answered the question. JP was unaware there was a football match being played in Turin that night.

"So, not the match, not a holiday obviously and no Rhoda."

"Rhonda."

"No, Rhonda. So it's a business trip."

"I'm retired, like you, I imagine."

"I'm still working. Retirement doesn't suit me. I like to keep myself occupied. Got to pay for the season ticket somehow."

That statement sounded nearer to the truth for JP. Malcolm looked like someone who needed to work rather than doing so for other reasons than paying bills.

"What do you do?" asked JP, wondering what Malcolm may have made of his life.

"I'm in retail distribution," he answered, grabbing a glimpse of his phone.

"Transport and logistics?"

"No, retail distribution is shops. You know, footfall, sales." He picked up his phone and examined it as if he was a high-flying executive.

"And what do you do in retail, Malcolm?"

"I'm at the sharp end. Front of house, as they say."

"And they kept you on after retirement?"

"There is no retirement anymore, John Paul. Age Discrimination Act sees to that. Now, what would you like to drink? Did you know that Turin is the Vermouth capital of the world?" The comment made it clear to JP that Malcolm had both read and experienced the Lonely Planet.

"I'll have another glass of this lovely Barolo if that's okay."

"No problem," came the reply, although the hesitancy in his voice suggested there might be when the bill arrived.

JP had already concluded that Malcolm didn't want to talk about marriage or work, which suggested that both might be areas where his old university friend didn't receive an A-star grade. JP couldn't recall meeting Malcolm after leaving university but asked him in case he was mistaken.

"No, I don't think we have," he answered.

"Nor, Rhonda, I imagine."

"No, I haven't seen Rhonda either," admitted Malcolm, snatching another glance at his mobile phone.

The action strangely disturbed JP. He wondered who his old friend was expecting to receive a call from. Perhaps it was Rhonda. If Malcolm was Rhonda's mysterious lover, then, of course, his old friend wouldn't admit to meeting her after university. Things that didn't fit began to fit perfectly in his mind.

Every step in this world was now related in some way to Rhonda's disappearance. And every person he met could have been her lover.

"So, you've never bumped into Rhonda?"

Malcolm shook his head. "No, not sure I'd recognise her now."

JP took a deep breath and interrogated himself. Had Malcolm seen his wife in his travels? Was he in touch with her in the years just after university? Did he meet her around 1979, a couple of years after they married? It seemed a strange coincidence that Malcolm should appear in one of the places JP hoped to find his wife. Could it possibly have been Malcolm she had an affair with?

Not sure he would recognise her? Why make a comment like that? He recognised me, thought JP.

Suspicion grew. He had evenly mispronounced her name. Rhoda, indeed, that was just a red herring.

"You didn't meet her again back in the late seventies or early eighties?"

"I don't think so, Old Man."

A photograph was placed on the table, which rather took Malcolm aback. Why was his old university friend carrying a photo of his wife around with him?

"Oh, yes, I recognise her now. Rhonda." He so wanted to ask why JP had a photo of her on his person. Not a small one in the back of his wallet, but one that barely fitted in the inside pocket of his jacket. He didn't know how to raise the question, so he changed the subject. He lifted up a small carrier bag and showed the contents to JP.

"It's for my granddaughter Sophie. She's ten. It's a Juventus football shirt with Morata's name on it. She'll love it."

"He's a footballer, I assume?"

"Morata? He's the Juventus centre forward. A great Spanish player."

JP was tempted to ask what Morata was doing in Italy but didn't. Instead, it fell to Malcolm to ask a question.

"So, what are you doing in Turin then?"

JP was reluctant to discuss his reason for being in Italy and wriggled off the hook with a question about the football match.

Fortunately, Malcolm liked talking about football. Eventually, JP got his long-lost friend on to the subject of his own wife rather than Rhonda. Somehow, Malcolm had assumed JP and his wife were having separate holidays. After all, surely he would have said if they had broken up.

"My wife would never agree to separate holidays. She hated me going to Spurs home matches every other week. I reckon she may have been a closet West Ham fan because suddenly it all changed. A couple of years ago she bought me a season ticket for my birthday. Spurs, not West Ham," he laughed. "I never knew she loved me so much. Then, five years ago, just when things seemed to be going so right, they became so wrong, and last year we got divorced. It was a Sunday, the 20th of August. We'd just lost to Chelsea at Wembley, and I returned home to find a note from my wife."

JP could not be sure which of those two events hurt him the most.

"She wanted me out of the house by the time she returned from her mum's place. A clean break, she called it."

"No warning?"

"We'd had separate beds for a while and different friends, I suppose. So that we might remain friends. Or, at least, that's what she said. She thought the situation was getting worse. Damage limitation she called the separation. You know, end it before it became too embittered."

"Was there anyone else? You know, a lover?" asked JP.

"No! Well, at least not then."

"And now?"

"Oh, there is now. I don't think my wife could live alone, hence the not liking me going to football, or not wanting separate holidays."

"And did the damage limitation work? Do you still get on?"

"Oh, not really. I don't see much of my ex anymore, except some family gatherings like Sophie's birthday."

"Have you got someone else?"

"No."

"Did your wife know the other fellow? The man she's with now?" JP sounded very interested in the relationship issue. It was a selfish question. He was still mulling over the risk of Rhonda leaving him for another man, perhaps the man she had an affair with back in the late seventies.

"Not really. Well, sort of. The bloke was our window cleaner. I only saw him occasionally because he cleaned our windows on a Saturday, and I was watching Spurs every other week."

JP was anxious to ask the following question but didn't know how to phrase it. Malcolm's absence on the day his wife had her windows cleaned seemed to provide the perfect opportunity for an adulterous affair. An open window effectively. JP finally asked his question, structuring it in almost medieval terminology.

"Your wife, Malcolm, I don't mean to be unkind, but could she be considered a loose woman?"

Malcolm thought about the question. The delay was not to consider his wife's guilt or otherwise. But he realised that answering such a question too quickly condemned the poor woman.

"Loose?" He finally queried. "Well, she certainly came undone quite easily at parties. She was fond of a drink."

JP chose to abandon the subject. "2014 was a good year for us," he commented reflectively.

"That's when Rhonda and I were last here, in Turin. Two centre holiday it was, Turin and Saluzzo. One week of sightseeing and another of rest and relaxation."

"2014 was a terrible year," declared Malcolm.

JP ran possible events through his head. Eight years ago, Malcolm's granddaughter would have been two years old, and his wife was probably depressed at being at home alone now that her own daughter had left home. Any marriage would come under pressure. That's perhaps when the problems began. It made complete sense, but he had to ask why that particular year was so wrong. JP soon regretted seeking such clarification.

According to Malcolm, England was knocked out in the group stages of the World Cup in Brazil. And Spurs finished outside the European places in the league. It soon became apparent that Malcolm saw his life through his time's major sporting events and sporting personalities.

"My dad took me to so many major sporting events when I was a kid. We went to the World Cup Final in 1966. We were at Highbury when Muhammed Ali beat Henry Cooper."

Malcolm added several more sporting events, compass points in his narrow life. Not personal moments, like getting married or kids being born, but times he spent with his dad and more recently on his own, watching football matches and other events.

To JP, the crucial moments of life were small, seemingly unimportant events. Indeed not children being born or special birthdays.

We are not defined by age or our children, or indeed our father, he thought to himself as he listened to Malcolm's ramblings. Our children may be defined by us. And yes, his own father certainly influenced him. He would be the first to admit that. But life's turning points are just that. They consist of turning right one day instead of left, and it is not as if we actually remember turning right.

"Where is your wife?" Malcolm suddenly asked.

"My wife?" JP hesitated, and this time, he looked at Malcolm's mobile phone, lying dormant on the table, hoping it would ring. "Rhonda wanted a more relaxing holiday, so she went directly to Bellagio from our short stay in Nice. I'm travelling via Turin. Catch up on some sightseeing." He failed to mention Cuneo and Saluzzo.

"How long are you away for?"

"Three weeks."

"Strange, isn't it? My wife would never consider separate holidays, and now we're living separate lives."

"We're not on a separate holiday," responded JP a little too defensively.

"Yes," Malcolm continued, talking to himself as much as JP. "Five years ago, we split up, in September, actually. The 12th of September 2017."

God, thought JP, he remembers the actual day his wife went her own way. Even an unfeeling, indulgent individual like Malcolm remembers the day he lost his wife. Malcolm was still talking. JP felt a rash of guilt as he recognised he couldn't remember when his wife had left him.

"I'm not sure I'm cut out for being single. I miss married life more than I miss my wife. We're all snails or slugs, aren't we?"

"Snails or slugs? Are we?" questioned JP.

"There are snails, and there are slugs," he repeated. "Snails like homes and slugs like their freedom. But they are equally at the mercy of others, similarly vulnerable. One thinks itself safer, more secure than the other," Malcolm said knowingly. "None of us is safe. We just convince ourselves otherwise."

Malcolm's philosophical lament went directly into a similar elegy on what was wrong with professional football in the modern era.

"We're missing a Clough or a Shankly," he told JP. "Or a Nicholson," he added out of loyalty to his favoured team. "Football managers aren't managers anymore. They're coaches."

JP saw a tiny thread of symmetry in the subject matter, enough to divert the conversation away from football.

"Do you know the UK has five million managers?"

"Football managers?" asked Malcolm.

"No, managers in a business. Company managers. Ten years ago, it had just one-tenth of that, and just over a hundred years ago, the position didn't exist. There were no managers."

Malcolm was wondering how a football club would cope without a manager.

"We have thirty million people working in the UK," continued JP unhesitatingly. "And one in six is a bloody manager. Only five out of six people are doing any work. The job didn't exist until the railways arrived."

Any symmetry was lost on Malcolm.

"What is it you did before retiring, John?"

"I taught commerce and business studies at sixth form college. Looking back, it's clear Rhonda had the more difficult job. Bringing up kids isn't easy."

"Bringing up kids isn't about changing them. It's about changing yourself," countered Malcolm, reciting something he had read in a self-help guide.

Life has to be about something other than self, thought JP. Indeed that's what makes us human, a self-conscious entity. It occurred to JP that it was unlikely he would ever see Malcolm again. After all, he hadn't bumped into him in the last forty years. So, it seemed senseless to lie to him, and JP needed to share his feelings with someone. Well, someone other than Liza.

"Actually, Malcolm, I have a confession to make. Rhonda and I are not having separate holidays. My wife left me too. I have no idea why because she didn't leave a note. She just took her passport and clothes while I was at evening classes and left."

"Oh, I'm so sorry, John." He turned his body to look at his friend, wondering if he was about to cry.

"Strangely, she'd just been shopping. Why would she go shopping before leaving me? Why did she iron my shirts?"

"She still cared for you. That much is clear," offered Malcolm.

"She left me a packet of fish fingers. There must be a message in that, but I just can't work out what it is."

"Did you have a row?" The question stifled his voice.

"I don't think so. For all I know, she may have been kidnapped."

"Kidnapped? Who by, Captain Birdseye?" Malcolm regretted the joke, but JP hadn't heard it anyway. He was buried within himself, searching for a reason for Rhonda's departure.

"I'm looking for her. She probably just needs some time out. That's what they call it now, isn't it? Some space? Time out? They have that in football, don't they?" It was a generous, although poorly informed, invitation to Malcolm to join the conversation with something more than some sorrowful platitudes. "She said these were the best times of her life."

"What were?" Malcolm asked, picking up his phone again.

"Our holidays together," JP answered. "They were the best times of our life." He wandered into a reflective mood. "So that's where she would head off to, wouldn't she? It's logical. She'll be in Bellagio, her favourite place."

"Then why are you here?"

"I'm checking the other possibilities first."

"Why?"

"To rule them out. And to give Rhonda a little space, some time to think things through."

"You're afraid of finding her in case it's all over. That's the truth, isn't it, John?" He looked at his phone again.

JP shrugged, unconvinced by the statement. "Are you expecting a call?"

"No, I'm waiting for the team to be announced."

"Team?"

"The Spurs team for tonight's match." Malcolm switched subjects with ease. "It would help you to know why Rhonda left you. The usual reasons are infidelity or a violent husband." Malcolm spoke with the voice of experience.

"I could never be violent to Rhonda." He believed it possible of her. Not that she actually ever struck out at him. But there were times when she found her husband's pedantic behaviour frustrating.

"Have you tried any of the women's refuges? Or the Salvation Army?"

JP flinched at the thought.

"Where is it you live?"

"East Sussex, St Leonards, near Hastings."

"Oh, they'll be loads down there. Very liberal-minded people on the south coast. I mean, Southampton is the wife swapping capital of the UK and Brighton? Well, I'll say no more."

The suggestion was preposterous. Well-meaning but misguided, JP told himself. JP pushed his chair back noisily, intending to leave. But he couldn't insult the man. But he should have rebuked Malcolm because he was now speaking with increased conviction.

"Take domestic abuse," Malcolm continued at a pace.

"It's widespread, you know, especially on the south coast."

"What is?"

"Marital disharmony, domestic abuse in the fashion of poor Chantelle and Yasmeen. And then there's Helen."

Chantelle, Yasmeen? Who are these people, wondered JP? "Were they at Uni with us?"

"Uni? No, of course not. They're victims of domestic abuse. You must know about Chantelle and Gray, Yasmeen and Geoff. And then there's Helen and Rob. Who would have thought, eh, Helen and Rob?"

The names crawled slowly through JP's shallow memory, impeded by his inability to recognise any of them.

"I don't know a Chantelle Gray," he finally confessed.

"No, not Chantelle Gray," laughed Malcolm. "Chantelle and Gray. Gray Atkins was the abuser."

"And we knew them did we?"

"Knew them? No, of course not. I'm talking EastEnders and Corrie."

"Well, that's not real life, is it Malcolm?" JP sounded a little exasperated.

"It reflects real life, Ringo."

Nobody had called JP Ringo since his university days, but he ignored it anyway.

"But it's not real life, is it?"

"What about Helen then. The Archers, that's real life."

"No, it isn't. It's a radio programme."

"Well, it's as close to real-life as you can get."

Sensing that his long-lost friend may need to open his soul, JP hesitated with his next question.

"So, is that why your wife left you?"

"My wife didn't leave me," Malcolm insisted, taking umbrage at the suggestion. "We split up, got divorced. It was me who had to leave the family home. Now, that's what I call domestic abuse, forcing a man out of his home."

Malcolm could quite easily have continued his angry rant, but his phone buzzed and flashed with the impetuosity of a small child.

"Oh, I need to go, mate. I'm meeting up with the Spurs supporters at another bar." He hesitated, wondering how to best bring the conversation to an end. "I hope you find Rhoda, Ringo."

"Rhonda."

"Rhonda, yes. I hope you find her. Patch things up. You two were made for each other."

JP watched as Malcolm left the bar. He wanted to check which way he turned, not wanting to bump into him again during his wanderings around the city. Eventually, he found himself back at the hotel when his phone rang.

"Can I call you back in a moment, Liza?" he asked.

"Dad, stop avoiding me."

"I'm not avoiding you, darling. You know I don't like holding telephone conversations in public places. There's nothing worse than having to listen to someone telling his wife he will be home in twenty minutes and to put the sausages on."

"Well, promise you'll ring me back."

"I'm just about to get in the lift to head up to my room. I want to get changed before dinner. I'll call you in a few minutes. I promise."

Liza had been mulling over a comment on their previous conversation. Her father had said he would be staying in Turin for 'No more than two nights.' She knew her father planned his holidays down to the last detail and booked everything in advance. So 'no more than two nights' was a lie. And, if that was a lie, what other lies had her father been telling her?

JP went straight to the mini-bar when he got to his room. He needed something more substantial than a Barolo before he spoke to Liza. How could he politely tell her he needed some space of his own. If he had established anything from his wasted afternoon, it was that he needed some time alone. Her constant calling wasn't helping.

"Where are you?"

"I'm still in Turin. I told you I would be here for a couple of days. Oh, and I've just met an old friend from my university days."

"Oh, that was nice for you, Dad."

"He's only here for a football match. Apparently, there's one in the city tonight, but I'm not sure who's playing."

Liza waited for him to stop speaking. She had an important matter to discuss.

"You were going to text a password to me. The one to access your computer."

JP hadn't given any more thought to his daughter's request.

"Sorry, I've forgotten it. But it must be written down somewhere. I read you should change passwords regularly, so I do. I just can't remember them, so I write them down."

"Uh-huh! Where?"

"Where?"

"Where do you write the passwords down, Dad?" Her voice was becoming irritated.

"Oh, in the backs of books, places like that. Not my nice collectable ones, but not one I would throw away, of course."

"Right, so how will I know if I've found the right book? And how will I know it's the current password?"

"I'll give it some thought."

Liza had a plan. If she could keep her father talking for any length of time, then he might eventually slip up and tell her the details of his trip.

"Um! Dad? You know you said Mum was suing the gym?"

"Yes, dear."

"Well, I've been thinking about that." She paused to make sure he was listening. "Now, you said that you heard Mum on the phone, right? Are you sure she wasn't just talking about Sue, the woman who runs the gym? Did you not just hear her mention 'Sue in the gym'? Rather than 'suing the gym?'"

It went silent for a moment.

"Dad, did she just say 'Sue in the gym?'"

"Perhaps," he whimpered defeatedly.

"Uh-huh! Right, well, that's cleared up then. Now look, Dad, Lester is worried about you."

"Yes, you told me, Liza. But I'm not sure how you can tell. He never seems to demonstrate any emotions to me." Liza went to interrupt, but he continued releasing his inner thoughts. "He always appears like a poor, stray waif to me. He dresses so scruffily. Unkempt would be too kind. He always looks like one of those beggars you see outside railway stations. I often feel like pressing some cash into his hand. But, since Covid, there seems to be less cash around."

"Oh, don't worry, Dad, Lester accepts all major credit cards. Mine normally."

"I'm so sorry, darling, you're so kind. It should be me dealing with things like that. It's so tricky with your mum not being around."

"So, where are you off to next?" Her question sounded deliberately offhand.

"Ferrara," he answered unwittingly. He could almost hear her writing his answer down.

"Um! I know!" she announced in a celebratory voice, "I could meet you there. We could spend a few days together. When will you arrive in Ferrara, and how long are you staying?"

"Perhaps a little later, darling. I'm only going to be in Ferrara for a couple of days, maybe less. You won't get a flight in time to make it worthwhile."

What's less than a couple of days, wondered Liza?

"Hmm! Okay, where are you going after that? Or are you coming home?"

"Not sure at the moment. I tell you what, I'll let you know my plans when I get to Ferrara, and we can decide then."

Liza knew very well that her father would have planned the trip precisely. He would know the details of his next move. Being unsure of the next move was inconceivable to her father.

"Um! Is this about Mum? The trip, I mean. Is it about Mum?"

"Yes, dear."

"You need to come to terms with it, Dad."

"Yes, I know. I'm lost without your mum. And I can't simply sit at home doing nothing. You must understand that."

"Yes, I do," she answered, although, in truth, she understood very little about the current situation.

7

Ferrara, Emilia Romagna

Recalling his experience of booking a taxi through the hotel in Saluzzo, JP checked out of the hotel and walked to a nearby taxi rank for his transfer to the railway station. He was unsure of his reasons for doing this, but it allowed him time to practice his Italian. More importantly, it offered a few minutes to gather his thoughts.

Much to JP's annoyance, the structured organisation of British taxi ranks is lost on the Italians. Queuing is a very English thing, he assured himself. In most major cities at home, they almost unfailingly form a straight line. Some even provide a supervisor to marry the two parties amicably.

Yet, taxi ranks in Italy represent no more than a mere scattering of taxis waiting for fares. The heat ensures that drivers never remain in their cab, so identifying which one belongs to a particular taxi is the first challenge. Even if you throw a six to start, the second burden is to separate the one at the head of the queue from the others who are simply interested in holding a conversation. This conversation need not even be about where you want to go. Indeed it rarely is. This malleable arrangement presented particular difficulties for JP, who feared the ungodliness of disorder. For a moment, he stood panning the horde of itinerant workers. And he reflected, ruefully, on his decision not to use the hotel concierge.

"Dove?" a taxi driver screamed at him.

The question threw him because he already held a well-structured sentence in his head.

"Il Stazione," JP stuttered unhelpfully.

"Quale Stazione?"

Unbeknown to JP, there are two railway stations in Turin. One called Porta Nuova and the other called, somewhat confusingly, Eni.

"Eni?" asked one driver.

"Any? No, not any station. Torina stazione," he replied.

The taxi driver shook his head.

"Ferrara. I'm going to Ferrara."

The statement confused the driver.

"Dove?"

"Ferrara."

"Ferrara?" another taxi driver asks with great interest, thinking this will pay the rent for a week.

"Ferrara is four hundred kilometres," advises a third man speaking good English. A fourth colleague quickly converts the fare into euros.

"Three hundred euros," the first one confirms, rubbing his thumb and forefinger together.

Let's start again, thought JP. "Torino Stazione," he declared.

"There are two," explains the English-speaking driver. "If you are going to Ferrara, you need Porta Nuova. Andrea here will take you." He pointed to a somewhat overweight man with sweat running from every pore of his body who had shown little interest in the fare from the beginning.

He stubbed out a cigarette and swung himself into the driver's seat, leaving JP to throw his suitcase in the back.

If JP thought the taxi rank was disordered, he found it wanting compared to the railway station. Train passengers, like everyone else in Italy, demonstrate a wanton disregard for rules. It was less apparent on the little slow train from Nice to Cuneo. But, on the inter-city services, more regular commuters sit wherever they wish. Even the production of a ticket with a seat number on it has little effect. One has to wait until a ticket inspector or attendant appears to get someone to move. Even then, any complaint is often met with a dismissive shrug of the shoulders.

JP's love of Italy was marred by this single fact. His pedantic faith in systems and rules floundered when strapped to the mast of this hijacked ship of a train service. The mutineers do precisely as they please. And yet, despite this, he preferred rail travel to driving a car. Indeed, he shivered at the very thought of a car journey from Turin to Bologna.

This was not a last-minute change because JP had been thinking about it previously. He bought a ticket for Bologna rather than Ferrara. The train passed through Bologna, and there was just a chance that Rhonda might have chosen to stay here. The couple had never stayed in the famous city. However, they had visited it on two occasions, following a recommendation for a hidden treasure of a restaurant there.

The small Ristorante Al Sangiovese was named after the famous wine grape. The family that owned the place would undoubtedly know Rhonda, having presented her with a bottle of the wine she complimented so much on their second visit.

The owner recognised his unannounced customer immediately. "Mr Preparé, how are you?"

It was early, and there were no customers in the small restaurant. The owner took the suitcase and placed it in a space in one corner. He stood there for a moment, waiting for the man's wife to appear. JP could see that the owner was going to ask him where she was.

"You remember my wife?" asked JP, removing the photograph from his jacket.

"Of course." And he did genuinely recall her. JP could see that in his sincere expression.

"And where is your good lady wife?"

"We've become separated. And she has lost her phone." JP's voice was hesitant because it was filled with remorse at his attempt at lying again. He didn't want to malign her name in front of the owners as he was sure he would be returning here with Rhonda in the not-too-distant future. "We're staying in Ferrara. I just wondered if she had been in here?"

The owner and his wife exchanged glances, relieved that Mrs Preparé had not passed from this world.

"No, we have not seen your wife today, Mr Preparé."

"Yesterday?" JP asked hesitantly, "or recently?"

The owner looked confused. "When did you become separated?" There was sincere concern in the man's voice.

JP's last statement, asking if they had seen her recently, did not sit well with the story he had told. His hesitation wasn't helping the situation.

"I'm not sure. I forget things lately. Dates get mixed up a little. But recently, yes, we became separated."

Now the proprietor looked extremely concerned. He wondered whether to call the police. His wife appeared.

"Do you want us to call someone for you, Mr Preparé? Did your wife not return to the hotel?"

"You're right," JP declared. "I should go to the police. I'll do that." He stepped around a table and lifted his suitcase. "I'll do that right now. That's a good suggestion. Yes. Thank you for your help."

He left the owners distraught by his meandering explanation of his missing wife. They discussed whether to contact someone to make sure he was alright. But they didn't, and JP didn't go to the police, of course. It was the railway station he went to instead. And as he walked there, he berated himself about the desperate situation he had caused. He really needed to produce a more convincing story if he was going to find Rhonda.

As the train drew closer to Ferrara, JP's hopes of finding his wife in the medieval walled city grew increasingly palpable. He was not surprised she did not go to Nice, Cuneo, Saluzzo, Turin, or even Bologna. Indeed, by now, he had convinced himself that she would not go to Bellagio either. Rhonda knew that Bellagio was where JP would look for her. And it would be simple to find her in such a small town. If she was serious about not being located, she would go to a large city, where her anonymity could be assured. It would be one she was familiar with, like Ferrara. His brief visit to Bologna convinced him that the hordes of tourists visiting cities like that one or Florence would not provide the quiet retreat she needed to escape from this busy world. The ancient walled city of Ferrara was perfect to lose oneself and to isolate from the world.

After his failure to produce a credible story about his missing wife to the barman at the Turin hotel and to the owners of Al Sangiovese restaurant, JP decided to change the narrative of Rhonda's disappearance.

As the taxi approached the hotel, JP looked at his mobile phone. He pressed it to his ear and listened. 'Hi, this is Rhonda,' the voice told him. 'Please leave a message, and I'll call you back.' He sat there looking at the phone until the driver pulled up outside the hotel.

Checking in to Hotel Annunziata, it was nice to see a familiar face. JP had seen a few on this trip, but few seemed to recognise him. Well, not the way that Giovanni recognised him as he walked through the hotel doors

"Buona sera, Mr Preparé. Come stai?"

"Non ce male, Giovanni," JP answered.

The young man laughed at the expression. Not too bad. His unchanged features gave JP a comfortable feeling.

His kind face made Giovanni the least intimidating of men. He was attentive without being condescending. However, the front desk clerk could quickly paint you into a corner with his persistent questioning. If JP hoped to enlist the man's help without revealing any information himself, he was sorely wrong.

"My wife left home, ran off."

"Why?"

Giovanni was a quiet man, almost to the point of being repressed, but never depressed and always full of questions. The amiable desk clerk quickly learned that JP's wife had debts caused by a shopping habit.

"She has BSD," confessed JP, who had read about the problem online during the train journey. "Buying Shopping Disorder," he explained.

Giovanni listened attentively as JP explained that any recovery would only be possible by first admitting that she had a problem. This first step is always the same in such disorders, JP told him. Alcoholism, gambling all require the person to admit to having the problem.

"Is there no help available?" asked Giovanni.

"There's a self-help group."

"What do they suggest?"

Every statement JP made was countered with another question. JP just wanted to know if Rhonda had been seen in town. He tried to scream and did so internally.

"They encourage you to make lists for shopping, don't graze, and get rid of all credit cards. Compulsive Buying Disorder has manic episodes like bipolar. Holidays prove a difficult time. There are too many shops, you see." He paused. "It is a recognised medical disorder." He was rambling now, reciting what he had memorised from the magazine he read on the train.

"Bipolar?" questioned the hotel clerk.

"There are many different types of similar problems."

JP tried to remember those he had read up on before deciding on BSD. "Alice in Wonderland Syndrome, where people have a problem dealing with reality. Cotard's Syndrome is where a person thinks they're dead. And Capgras delusion is a frightening disorder where the sufferer believes that a close personal friend has been replaced by an imposter."

Giovanni's expression changed with each condition JP related to him.

"Paris Syndrome," JP continued without hesitating. "This affects primarily Japanese tourists. Paris syndrome is where someone visits the city and is highly disappointed in what they find."

"Which city?" asked Giovanni.

"Well, Paris, I suppose."

"And your wife, she is still suffering from this BSD?"

"Yes, she continues to make ridiculous purchases.

She went out to buy dinner one day and came back with a kennel." JP was now moving on to the examples of BSD he had read about. He was sure this was reinforcing the solid back-story he had created.

"What's wrong with buying a kennel?"

"We don't have a dog."

"Then why did she buy the kennel?"

"It was half price," answered JP, thinking quickly and trying to recall some other examples.

"She bought a lifetime subscription to a wrestling magazine. It's called Oniomania, or compulsive shopping. It's become an acceptable addiction like victimless crimes."

Giovanni was speechless. He had finally run out of questions.

"Have you seen my wife?" JP asked him, placing the photograph on the counter along with his passport.

"No, not since you last visited us together, Mr Preparé." The desk clerk's interest was waning, but the conversation was not.

JP wrenched himself away from the attentive Giovanni and headed off to his room. Another hotel room, another en-suite bathroom, and another mirror to practice what he will say when he meets Rhonda. JP unpacked and went into that bathroom. And glancing sideways at the mirror, he began talking. "I don't want you to come home," he announced with a rueful smile. It was a trick he used in class to get the students' attention. "Not if you don't want to. But, if you do want to, then arrangements could be made."

JP looked down at the floor and shook his head. "No, no, no, no, no," he shouted a little too loudly, realising he was overcooking the attention-grabbing introduction. When the opportunity arrives, it may only last a few minutes, he told himself. He rested Rhonda's photograph on the shelf next to the sink.

"Look, this may sound stupid," he told her. "But then I forget so much lately. So I'll just say this straight out. I do love you, and I don't know when it was that you stopped loving me. All I'm sure of is that you don't love me. Otherwise, you wouldn't have left. And I know this because I couldn't leave you."

What would he say next if she hadn't responded?

"I looked at a house in Drummond Road the other day. Not looking at it in the sense of viewing the property, you understand. I just looked at it. I could move there, out of your way. I'm not sure I could go further than Drummond Road. Not like you, running off to Italy." The last remark sounded vindictive, too unforgiving.

JP abandoned his rehearsal, showered and changed. He and Rhonda had only ever stayed in the Hotel Annunziata when visiting Ferrara, so she would have stayed here. Or would she?

Of course, he told himself. If her husband did, by chance, look for her in Ferrara, then, of course, she would not stay in the same hotel they had been to before.

She might be in a different hotel, but she would visit the same restaurants and bars they went to. His conviction that Rhonda was in Ferrara was undiminished by Giovanni's negative response.

The renaissance city of Ferrara has a remarkable cultural history, an ancient kingdom that sits not far from the wetlands of the Po Delta. Like Saluzzo, the city has a defensive wall built in the 12th century. Over time, this medieval town was extended to accommodate urban growth, and today the walls encircle the medieval city, the Cathedral of San Giorgio and the Estense Castle. JP felt entombed by a circle of fading memories. He would walk around the walls of the city tomorrow.

Their last visit to Ferrara was in 2011 when Prince William got married to Kate Middleton. Rhonda was annoyed at missing it. "We haven't been invited," JP joked. Instead, they watched the Palio that is held in the Piazza Ariosto each May.

The spectacle and pageantry were equal to a royal wedding at home, but there is little romance in the Palio itself. The brutal horse race resulted in injured horses and jockeys following a crash on one of the sharp bends around the converted dust track of the Piazza Ariosto. Rhonda and JP promised to return for the other elements of the medieval ceremony, the flag-throwing, the playlets and the procession itself.

Not surprisingly, the staff at the Leon d'Or café and bar did not recognise JP. Nevertheless, they plied him with an endless supply of vol-au-vents, olives and nuts to accompany his glass of Prosecco. The tables at the front of the building run along the pavement, covered by an awning. It reminded him of Renoir's *Luncheon of the Boating Party*, a crowd of people huddled beneath the flapping white canvas. The tables were so close to each other it was impossible to separate oneself from the other customers.

An American tourist on the adjacent table appeared to be travelling alone. He sat drinking a rust-coloured spirit which he topped up with Coke from time to time. He was about ten years younger than JP and smiled when they exchanged glances.

When JP took a photograph from his jacket pocket and placed it on the table, the American straightened his chair a little and feigned a distracted look along the row of tables. He mentioned the weather to JP, who told him it was much cooler in England.

"It's forty-five degrees in Phoenix," came the response.

"Have you been in Ferrara long?" JP asked. It seemed pointless to ask if the man had seen Rhonda if he had only arrived today.

"About a week. This city is convenient for travelling around the region. You can go by train from Ferrara to Venice, Bologna, Ravenna. The only place it doesn't connect with is Modena. I wanted to see where Pavarotti came from."

The man spoke about himself for ten minutes, not once asking JP anything about himself. It soon became apparent that here was a man with entrenched certainties about life, both generally and psychologically. He held views on many subjects, perhaps all subjects. He spoke about the power of positive thinking and the need to maintain an optimistic outlook on life. Any harmful elements of his life had been blasted with dopamine as soon as they appeared. He wasn't a psychiatrist himself, but he had seen one – well, several, it seems, because there appeared to be several remedies for his particular condition.

When he eventually showed an interest in the photograph, JP decided to keep the back-story as simple as possible. They had an argument, and she'd left.

"Do you talk to your wife?"

"Not since she left."

"No, I mean, do you really talk to her? Talking is an essential part of the relationship, you know."

JP did know.

"It's the key to a healthy relationship. Make time for one another and talk. Not about the kids or money. You need to talk about your emotions, more profound issues. Get up close and personal. Arrange date nights and don't let the sex become boring. Watch some porn together."

"Look, I've got to be somewhere," JP stated, disturbing the man's unending flow of advice.

"Where are you going? Perhaps I can tag along."

"I'm meeting someone."

"Whoa," the American boomed. "Well, there you go, buddy. Your wife's only been gone a couple of days, and you're already fooling around. Now you have to ask yourself the question."

JP stood up, thanked the gentleman for his advice, and went inside to settle the bill. There was an outdoor restaurant at the rear of the building, which provided another exit. JP took it and made his way down a tiny alley by the side of the cathedral to a small bar used mainly by students. The large wooden tables were a little more spaced out here, but their size meant solitary drinkers would need to share their space. He claimed the last remaining empty table, which had eight chairs around it.

The only waiter was busy serving drinks, and by the time he got to JP, three young women had sat at his table. JP tried to ignore their giggling, although he made several attempts to translate their conversation, all without success. He dipped his head into the wine list until the waiter arrived.

"Ha una vini chiama Conde?"

The waiter looked a little confused by his poor translation. "Hai un vino chiamato Conde?" asked one of the women.

JP smiled, and the waiter repeated the name Conde to him.

"Yes, do you have a wine called Conde?"

"Riserva or Superiore?"

"Riserva," answered JP.

"And how many glasses do you require," the waiter asked in almost perfect English.

The girls all laughed and exchanged whispered comments.

"Piace vino?" JP asked them.

"Vuoi un po 'di vino," replied one, correcting him.

JP had given up trying to translate responses but took it as a positive answer. "Quattro bicchieri per favore," he told the waiter.

The three women thanked him for his generosity.

"Are you sure?" asked one.

"It's my pleasure," he smiled. "It's a lovely wine and should be shared. Anyway, one shouldn't drink on their own. It isn't good form." The words didn't translate easily into Italian.

The waiter returned with the bottle and four large bowl glasses. As they waited, JP pulled the photograph from his pocket and placed it on the table before asking the women if they had seen his wife. The question caused each of them to examine the stranger in more detail. He didn't look like a bullying husband, although they could not be sure what had caused his wife to run away. Their reluctance to answer gave JP false hope. Perhaps they had seen her and were unsure about sharing that information with him. He thought quickly about how he might persuade them of his good intention.

"Our dog ran away during our holiday, and my wife insisted on returning to Italy to look for him." A lost pet portrayed a much different scenario than simply a husband searching for his runaway wife. It worked, and the table flooded with empathy, which the American visitor at the Leon d'Or would have appreciated.

But it was all to no avail as the women had not seen Rhonda. They were also surprised and a little concerned that JP did not carry a photograph of the dog with him. No wonder his wife left him if he cared so little about a poor, lost dog.

"What was the dog's name?" one of them asked.

The hesitation in JP's response spoke volumes. And, in those lost seconds, he heard a woman on the next table order a bottle of J2O.

"OJ," answered JP.

"You named your dog," one of the young women stuttered in a tone mixed with contempt and incredulity, "after that wife killer, OJ Simpson?"

"I have a table booked for dinner," explained JP as he stood up to leave. But at that very moment, the cavalry arrived in the shape of Giovanni, who had just finished his shift. The hotel desk clerk was somewhat surprised to find his newly arrived guest in the company of three much younger women. Still, delicacy dictated that he ignored the dubious situation.

"I had an idea about the problem with your wife, Mr Preparé," Giovanni said as he paused to exchange pleasantries. The three women looked up eagerly. "Have you thought about selling the kennel on eBay?"

There was a sharp intake of breath from the young women, who stood up and left hurriedly, screeching and talking as they departed.

When JP arrived at La Providenza restaurant for dinner, he felt terribly guilty telling such stories about his wife.

In future, he would simply put the photograph on the table and silently invite comments. If asked, he would say Rhonda had an affair and ran away, unable to face the music. Love's unshared thoughts he would refer to it. Marriage is the product of true love. And true love is wanting to spend your life with someone who wants you in their life too. But Rhonda no longer wanted JP in her life. That was the simple truth of the matter. If she is looking for peace and quiet and perhaps space to think things through, maybe then she wouldn't have come to Ferrara. But then, for the same reason, that would rule out Rome, Florence and Venice.

Sitting alone at dinner anywhere in the world, whether it be in the noisy capital of Rome or the serene surroundings of Bellagio, was unbearable.

Suddenly Nervi came to mind for no other reason than a momentary thought about his parents. They died the year Rhonda and JP went to the small seaside resort in Liguria, and they yearned for somewhere for quiet reflection. Their minds conjured up the innocent pleasures of a small fishing village on the coast. Nervi fitted the bill perfectly, perched midway between Portofino and Genoa. The proper description was remote, at least then, back in 2004. It has probably changed now, JP convinced himself. The Italians loved a seafront and thought nothing of sunbathing on rocky beaches. The following year was JP's attempt at a two-centre holiday with the first week in Florence and the second in the resort of Montecatini, with its thermal baths and the wonderful hilltop town of Montecatini Alto. They had done Sorrento by then and been put off by the Britishness of venues like the Foreigner's Club, with its swarm of ex-pats. And after Montecatini came Mantua and Modena.

On reflection, he would have enjoyed a long genial discussion with a fellow traveller on the attraction of Pavarotti's home town. Ideally, that fellow traveller would be Rhonda, but certainly not the American tourist he bumped into at Leon d'Or.

JP's parents died between his and Rhonda's twenty-fifth and thirtieth wedding anniversaries, both of which were enjoyed in Bellagio. As JP finished his main course and refilled his glass from the decanter, he sensed he would find his wife in Bellagio. He rejected any idea of looking for Rhonda in Nervi. That entire holiday had been a disappointment, just a silly dream about going to a small isolated fishing village. It is what it said on the tin, he thought. Remote, primitive even, but not as primitive as Italy was when they first visited the country in the early nineties. Then, most public toilets were just holes in the ground.

He paid the bill and picked up the photograph from the table. Nobody had asked about its significance. And he was reasonably sure he had not been recognised, despite several visits in previous years. No, he convinced himself. Rhonda is not in Ferrara. She must be in Bellagio. She wasn't really hiding, and perhaps she even wanted to be found. There were just two places to check out on the way, and both were possibilities.

Mantua because it was not unlike Ferrara, full of history. And yet, the accommodation in Mantua was not a hotel like the Annunziata. It was an apartment, perhaps much more suited to a single traveller like Rhonda. And if his wife wasn't there, he would proceed to the small lakeside town of Orta San Giulio, another city not unsuited to a person travelling alone.

8

Mantua

The constant hum of traffic and the distant sound of an ambulance siren died as JP stared inattentively out of the car window. The world was momentarily excluded from his thoughts, and he could have been travelling between kingdoms in the Middle Ages. He closed his eyes and recalled previous visits to time-trapped cities with Rhonda after the children grew up. Mantua is a unique city and, like Ferrara, a cultural hub of the Renaissance. The stout defences of such towns say much about the cruelty of that era. Ancient Italian cities are walled like Ferrara and Lucca or built on hilltops like Taormina and Assisi. But it is water that protects Mantua. Lakes and rivers provide the natural defences of a moat that surrounds the city of the Gonzaga family.

The rose-tinted memories of holidays with Rhonda took him back to Rome, a city they visited often.

On the first such visit, they attended a papal audience with thousands of others. John Paul II rode like the pale body of El Cid on his Popemobile around the gathered masses in his final years. The second trip was in 2000. Rhonda wanted to obtain a plenary indulgence. And this, despite the many and varied prerequisites to escaping purgatory, not least of which was being a Catholic. Eyes closed, the train click-clacking along, JP laughed inwardly.

The journey from Ferrara to Mantua takes just over two hours by train, but for JP, it was shorter because he got off at the little-known city of Suzzara. Passengers for Mantua have to change here anyway. But JP wanted to enter the city of the Gonzaga dynasty by car. Suzzara is referred to as a commune but was given honorary city status. It is effectively a key suburb of Mantua and home to a large Iveco factory. Because of its many business travellers, there is a busy taxi rank at the station. One driver was pleased to get a fare to Mantua.

The sweeping approach into Mantua across its moated defences is majestic. JP might have imagined what it was like to be a member of the Gonzaga family who ruled this place for four hundred years. But instead, he thought about Rhonda, wondering what he would do if he could not find her.

The driver explained that he was not permitted to stop in the Piazza Sordello. He phoned the Palazzo Castiglione and requested them to open the gates to allow him entry. The Castiglioni is not a hotel but a complex of suites, so few staff are around. JP seized his opportunity to show one member the photograph of his wife when he checked in. She had not seen Rhonda.

It was cool inside the historic Palazzo Castiglioni, and his room was spacious enough to produce an echo. After unpacking, JP went outside into the hot afternoon sun and wandered about the unshaded Piazza Sordello. It was too early for a gin and tonic, and the intense heat prompted him to seek the shade of the Basilica di Sant Andrea where he could relax in its consecrated coolness. Sitting in a church considered ordinary by Italian standards but exceptional in most parts of the world, he felt strangely close to Rhonda, as if she was sitting somewhere nearby. Conscious of his fading memory, JP suspected the condition may be more than the forgetfulness that comes with old age. He sensed he had passed beyond that particular forest's edge and wandered through the shrub and herb layers into its midmost trees. The retired teacher had suspected for some time that his memory was now only marginally illuminated by flickering sunlight through the canopy of a forgotten past.

JP gazed towards the altar. He had taken to reciting the night-time prayers of his childhood, puzzled by his capacity to recall the words from such distant past times. *He rued his strange powers of recall and the barbed variance in his inability to remember when Rhonda had left home. Now I lay me down to sleep, I pray the Lord my soul to keep. If I should die before I wake, I pray the Lord my soul to take.*

The prayer of his childhood rang of innocence and naivety. He adapted it in more recent times. He only ever prayed for one thing now, an incongruous soul-destroying plea to the Almighty. *Heavenly Father, my day is drawing to an end, and I'm ready to turn in. But before I do, I ask one thing. Take my soul before Liza, Lester and Rhonda.* At face value, it sounded selfless. A plea to take his life before the other members of his family. But, in truth, it was no more than selfish supplication because he couldn't face living without any of them. He couldn't bear the thought of laying any of them in the ground before he, himself, passed from this world.

When her father failed to check in with her for two days, Liza phoned the Turin hotel. She learned that Mr Preparé had checked out.

"Yes, I saw your father during his stay with us. I booked his table for dinner at Ristorante del Cambio when he checked in. He was travelling alone." The voice went quiet, and Liza wondered if she had been disconnected. Just as she went to speak, the clerk said. "He told us he had lost his wife."

"Um! Yes," answered Liza. "He told you, did he?"

"Yes, he showed us her picture."

Liza chose to ignore the remark. "And did he tell you where he was going to next?"

"No, I'm afraid not. Mr Preparé didn't ask me to call a taxi."

"Um! Did he mention Ferrara?"

"No, Madam."

She decided to call her brother, who answered the phone a little sleepily.

"Oh, hi, Liza. Is Dad back from France yet?"

"Hmm! He's not in France," she answered, but Lester didn't hear as he hadn't quite woken up yet.

"What is it with the French thing," a yawning voice asked. "Jean-Paul, Jean-Henri."

"Grandad was proud of his French ancestry," his sister answered. "All the first sons in the family were called Jean-Something."

"So why am I Lester then?"

"Because your grandfather wasn't your father. The idea of naming the firstborn with a French name rather came off the rails, a bit like you, Lester."

"Actually, most of my mates call me Les. It avoids a question and answers session on where the name Lester came from."

Grandad will be spinning in his grave, thought Liza.

"I didn't know that," she answered a little lazily.

"What, that my mates called me Les?"

"No, I didn't know you had any mates."

The comment woke her brother from his half slumber. "Yes, very funny."

"No, seriously, Lester, I don't know any of your mates."

"Why would you?"

"I'm your sister. Anyway, never mind about mates. Is there a girlfriend?"

"No. There's no such thing anymore."

"Um! You know what I mean. Is there someone in your life?"

"You mean am I sleeping with somebody? Male or female."

"That's not the most convincing riposte."

"Actually, riposte says a lot about your view of homosexuality and sexual liberation in general."

"Uh?"

"Yes, appalled, threatened."

"I am neither appalled nor threatened by homosexuality."

"But you're not indifferent to it."

"Nobody is indifferent to it,"

"Now, that speaks volumes about your position on the subject."

"What? Indifference?"

"Yes, that you think it's impossible to be indifferent about sexual liberation."

"I just think you're either gay or you're not."

"It's not black and white, Liz. It's everything in between."

"In your opinion. And stop calling me Liz. You might be okay with Les, but my name is Liza. Now, is there anyone in your life?"

"Yes, I suppose there is. Well, there are two people in my life now. Tabatha just had a baby."

"Your's?"

"Tabatha says the baby belongs to no one. It's not chattel. Oh, and it's not a he or a she."

"Chattel? Your girlfriend sounds quite Victorian. Dad will love her. What's the baby's name?"

"Girl-A."

"Well, that's a bit of a giveaway, isn't it?"

"It's called irony, Liza."

"So she actually calls the baby 'Girl-A', does she?"

"No, we call her Alpha for short."

"We? Is the baby yours, Lester?"

"I've already told you, Sis, the baby doesn't belong to anybody. Tabatha wants to ensure the baby doesn't suffer from gender dysphoria. Unconditional supportive mechanisms help the baby to become a fully functioning person."

"I think you'll find its feeding that does that. Look, Lester, are you the father?"

"The certificate says 'Father unknown'."

"Well, you have the right to know, don't you? So do I, come to that. I might be an auntie to this Girl-A, and I'd like to know for sure."

"Do you know what, Liza? Mum thought I called you Mona because you were enigmatic, you know, like the Mona Lisa. She didn't realise it was because you never stop moaning."

Moaning was how Liza secured the second bedroom, and Lester reminded her of the fact.

"I know Dad always thought it was an act of altruism on my part, but actually, it was for no other reason than to silence my moaning sister. It was always Moaner, not Mona."

"Yes, yes," Liza interrupted. "Dad's now gone to Ferrara, though God knows why. Have you given any more thought to the password?"

"What password?"

"God give me strength!" Liza shouted angrily. "The password to Dad's computer. We need to find out where he is going and what this Quixotic expedition is all about."

Lester recalled the previous telephone call from his sister. "Er, yes. It will be something to do with Mum or us. But most likely you. Try Liza Goddard."

"Look, I don't even know who Liza Goddard is, Lester. Why would his password be Liza Goddard?"

"Because that's who you're named after. Liza Goddard was famous – well, famous by today's standard. Today, even a singing window cleaner is famous. Liza Goddard appeared on *This is Your Life*. That's how famous she was."

"This is your what?"

"Oh, never mind. I'm not that much older than you."

"Um! Right, so Liza Goddard. Any other suggestions?"

"You could type in the letter L and see where it leads. Both our names start with the letter L."

"And where did your name come from?"

"Lester Piggott, I suppose. The famous jockey, though God knows why."

"So, Liza Goddard and Lester Piggott?" Liza was disappointed with her brother's contribution. "Right, well, I'm going over to Dad's house to see if I can get into the computer. Are you going to meet me there?"

"Why?"

"So we can find Dad together. Your father is wandering around Europe at the moment. Doesn't that worry you?"

"It makes me a bit envious, actually."

JP stepped back out into the burning sunshine of the early afternoon and made straight for the shade on the other side of the piazza. He wondered about visiting the Palazzo Ducal di Mantova which stood majestically away to his left, with its flowing pathways between rooms. But he couldn't be bothered with art today, so he strolled back round to the Bar Sordello. Its tables sprawled out onto the cobbled Piazza Sordello, each shaded with its own umbrella. Is it ever too early for a gin and tonic, he wondered?

The Castiglioni Suites didn't have any facilities, like a bar or dining room. So breakfast was taken at the Bar Sordello, which stood a few doors away in one corner of the square. The Bar Sordello was a rough spot and not the sort of place to order a Gin and Tonic. The only benefit of this was the alfresco experience impossible to find at home. The bar was a dishevelled sight in one of the most spectacular piazzas in Italy.

JP grabbed a swift glass of sparkling water and headed off to the nearby Bar Gonzaga for a proper drink. He stopped, on the way, at the Ristorante Grifone Bianco to book a table for dinner.

"Could I book a table for eight?"

"Eight?" The owner looked at the cloudless sky. "Of course, sir."

"Under the portico?"

"Certainly, Sir. And the name?"

JP was a little disappointed but realised the man could not be expected to remember the name of a customer who dined here once previously sixteen years ago.

"Preparé," he answered as he recalled that previous visit. "Do you still have the Agnoli pasta,"

The owner nodded his head and smiled, wondering if he had seen the man before.

"And the rabbit?"

"Si, certamente."

It had to be precisely the same, thought JP.

"And do you still have the Maurizio Zanella?"

"The Ca 'del Bosco? A beautiful wine, sir. Of course."

JP smiled and nodded enthusiastically.

"We will see you this evening, Mr Preparé."

JP turned away and then remembered something important. "Have you seen this lady recently?"

The owner looked closely at the photograph and shook his head.

"What about your wife?"

"She is out at the moment, Mr Preparé. Perhaps we can ask her this evening."

Liza met Robert during her voluntary work at the hospital. She had seen him around the wards. The orthopaedic registrar usually fixed people's broken bones but had been seconded to Covid-19 duties and looked after Ben during his final days. The funeral provided an opportunity to speak for the first time.

Apart from her brother, Robert was the only person Liza shared her feelings with. She told him of her father's suspicions about her mother's adulterous affair.

"My father told my mother that he didn't want to know the details. Is that normal, do you think?"

"If he doesn't know the details, then he can pretend it didn't happen."

"Pretend it didn't happen?"

"People deal with these things in different ways. What good would it do if he knew the person who had slept with his wife? He would almost certainly dwell on it."

"He forgave her, of course. On the condition that the affair was over, and she told him none of the details – not who, where, or when. And certainly not why."

"Well, there you are," replied Ben. "Each of these four elements of the affair haunted him, and the fewer details he knew, the easier it would be to forget."

"I'm just surprised that Mum didn't mention it to me. Especially if she told Dad. She shared everything with me."

"When was the affair?"

"Before I was born. In the first few years of their marriage, according to Dad."

"That isn't as unusual as you might think."

"I'm not sure it happened at all. But I'm just not sure why my dad would make such a thing up."

"Memory is a funny thing, Liza. You said he was becoming forgetful. It's the same principle. He just misremembers things."

"No, that can't be. How could you forget such a conversation? Anyway, she told him about it much later. Only a few years ago by the sound of it, perhaps even more recently."

JP showered and got dressed for dinner. He wondered about having a drink on the way to the restaurant but decided against it. It might spoil the taste of the Zanella, he told himself.

The owner, Massimo, welcomed JP and showed him to a massive table that sat under the shelter of the portico. For a moment, JP wondered if he would be sharing the table with other guests.

"Would you like a drink while you are waiting?"

The word waiting seemed a strange choice. Presumably, the comment meant waiting for his meal. He and Rhonda had a glass of prosecco the last time they came here. Perhaps he was referring to that.

"A bottle of the Maurizio Zanella, please." JP had given up speaking Italian. It seemed so pointless when the Italians spoke English so well.

Inside the restaurant, he could hear some other customers. Their muffled voices didn't make sense. Why was he sitting on a table laid for so many people? He resolved to overcome his embarrassment and ask Massimo when he returned. But he didn't need to.

"Will your other guests be having the red wine too?" Massimo asked.

"Other guests?" asked JP. "What other guests?"

"You ordered a table for eight people."

JP almost laughed but thought it might be inappropriate. Massimo might consider it a deliberate prank on his behalf.

"No, no," JP blurted. "I meant a table for eight o'clock, not a table for eight people."

Massimo laughed. "My apologies, sir. There is no need to book a time when reserving a table at Grifone Bianco. The table is yours for the whole evening."

"I'm so sorry," pleaded JP.

"No problem at all, sir," Massimo replied and immediately showed JP to another table set for two people further along the portico.

"I do apologise," JP continued saying as he took his seat.

Massimo retrieved the bottle of wine from the other table and poured a little into the glass for his breathless customer.

"Would you like to taste, sir?"

JP nodded, swished the wine around the glass and sipped it. Memories of their last visit here swept through his thoughts. Just as the smell of Rhonda's clothes produced evocative recollections, so did some wines. They were all in the company of Rhonda, with each wine a witness to the occasion.

JP sat, looking out on the large piazza, trying to catch his breath from the embarrassing situation. A cat made its way gingerly across the cobbles. It made him think about Blackie, although Rhonda's cat was only known by that name for the first year. It became unacceptable to call out the cat's name when it got dark. So she changed it to Lucky. "No, no," she told the kids. "His name was Lucky, not Blackie. You just misheard it." Lucky belonged to Rhonda and had little to do with JP.

The neighbours across the street used to look out for her when JP and Rhonda went on holiday. That week, the inappropriately named cat was run over by a car while Rhonda and JP were on holiday in Bellagio for the second time. The kids were still at junior school, and JP lied to them to avoid telling them that Lucky had died.

"She's gone back to her own mummy and daddy. She probably missed them."

"Can we go and visit her?" asked Liza.

"It's too far to go."

"Can't you use your fairy dust, Dad?"

Rhonda laughed when he came back down from Liza's bedroom. "Just tell them the truth," she suggested. Then came the lecture. She felt strongly about honesty. JP could remember her comments distinctly. Rhonda said he should embrace death as part of life, not the end of it.

Those words echoed about his thoughts as he conjured up the intoxicating fragrance of Rhonda. He could remember the way her eyes smiled before her mouth did. And he could never forget that shy glance away from any camera that might steal her spirit from this world. But his fading memory could not recapture her past beauty, of her university days. Nor, indeed, those happiest of times when the kids were too young to deter her flirting with him. Those vanishing memories are the essence of loss. He refused to believe she had disappeared forever. People do go missing, of course. We all go missing eventually, and in some distant time, we are all completely forgotten. Except for the very few, remembered only by those who did not know them - the historians and diarists. Liza tells him to be patient, but all forbearance is gone, departed along with any supply of fairy dust.

The restaurant began to fill up. Candles flickered under the portico at Grifone Bianco Restaurant, reminding JP of late evenings of the past. JP mourned the loss of such times. 'You should embrace death as part of life, not the end of it,' Rhonda whispered in his ear. He gazed towards the empty table set for eight people further along the portico and suddenly felt self-conscious of being alone. Still, the natural empathy of the other diners towards an old gentleman eating alone is universal. He sat quietly, his thoughts foraging for a moment in that past time where he and Rhonda were sitting enjoying a meal together. This particular memory was a more recent one, which worried him because it may have been the cause of his present state of affairs.

The word affairs rumbled like a bass drum. Why had he not thought of it before? An argument had almost certainly been the starting point. If he could remember the reason for the quarrel, he might understand her motive for leaving him.

What was the last disagreement they had? It would have been at home. They never argued in public, which would be far too unseemly. They would have been alone. They never raised their voices in front of the children. So they were at home, alone, discussing something which they disagreed upon. Money? He shook his head. It was not important enough for either of them to cause a row. Holidays? Unlikely, as she expected so little from their trips abroad.

Did she want to go back to Bellagio instead of Sicily? JP shook his head again. He finished his main course. "Delicious," he told the owner. "Un matrimonio fatto in cielo," smiled JP, but this seemed to confuse the man. "A marriage made in heaven," explained JP. The expression was obviously not used in Italy. "The wine and the meal," JP continued explaining. "They go perfectly together. Una combinazione perfetta."

"Ah," replied the owner. "Yes, the Maurizio Zanella and the braised donkey. Si, Stracotta D'Asino. It takes four hours to cook, bathed in red wine."

The words shocked JP, who was unaware he had chosen donkey. He believed he had ordered goat. Perhaps he should have requested the English menu. He groaned inwardly, a combination of guilt and disgust. The owner continued talking in English. He enjoyed a bottle of the Zanella recently with his wife. "On our anniversary," he added as he left carrying the plate where the donkey had been sacrificed in JP's name.

Anniversary thought, JP. Perhaps he had managed to forget their wedding anniversary? Quite the opposite was true, he convinced himself. He had ordered a bouquet of flowers four months before the date in case he forgot nearer the time. JP did not forget the date of his anniversary, but he did forget he had already ordered the flowers. On the day, two enormous sheaths of flowers appeared at the door.

"I love you twice as much as you think I do," was the best excuse he could find. Rhonda wasn't fooled. She knew exactly what had happened. She had noticed his forgetfulness and feared it might be something worse. There was a time when JP was sure of most things, then certainty waned to sureness. And that sureness lost confidence until he could no longer have faith in events of the past and how he remembered them.

Occasionally he would recall something she said, yet none provided a clue except, perhaps one when she commented on Bellagio. "If you could have only one holiday," she asked JP. "Where would you go?" He took too long to answer. "Somewhere different, or somewhere familiar?" she questioned him. He wasn't sure. "What about you?" he asked. Rhonda was not hesitant at all. "Bellagio, of course," she answered. Of course, he told himself, Rhonda has gone to Bellagio.

He thought for a moment about going directly to Lake Como rather than travelling via Lake Orta. But, what if he was wrong? If she wanted to be found, she would be in Bellagio. If not, then she might be in Orta.

The owner of Grifone Bianco returned to the table with his wife and placed the dessert menu in front of his guest.

"You wanted my wife to look at a photograph," he asked.

JP removed the photograph and gave it to the woman. He was only partially interested because nobody had recognised his wife in any of the places he had visited so far on the trip. He looked at the dessert menu, trying to translate it when the woman spoke.

"Penso di aver visto questa donna bere caffè nel bar Rigoletto." His wife didn't speak English, well, certainly not as well as her husband.

But she wasn't saying no. The tone in her voice made that much certain.

"My wife has seen this woman at the Rigoletto café. It is in Vicolo Gallo." He pointed off to the left.

His wife spoke again, and the man translated her words. "She drinks coffee there each morning." He didn't ask the purpose of JP's enquiry, nor did he question who the woman was in the photograph.

JP's heart began beating faster. He couldn't think about the dessert, so he asked for the bill and quickly finished his wine while he waited for it. He soon found Vicolo Gallo and the Rigoletto café. The staff were just closing up, and JP wondered whether he might show them the photograph. The temptation rose within him, but he just stood there watching them from across the street. If he asked about Rhonda, they might become suspicious and alert her of his presence in town.

He went back to his room and tried to sleep. Mantua, he wondered. Why had she come to Mantua? They hadn't been there for so many years. And, if she had been here for some time, why had she not returned to the Grifone Bianco Restaurant?

JP could barely contain himself the following morning. He showered, shaved and chose some smart clothes. Should he sit in the café and wait for her, or just stand nearby? He chose the latter and wandered along the street a few times, looking in the shop windows and trying not to appear furtive.

Just before ten o'clock, the woman arrived. He could understand how a person could be fooled. But it wasn't Rhonda.

He ventured into the café and sat as close to the woman as he could. She looked Italian, and she spoke the language fluently. Like Rhonda's, her skin was not pale but bordering on olive, her nose a little too thin, and her face too flat. And the blush in her cheeks was not delivered by nature but by cosmetics.

In a brief moment of hopefulness, he wondered if another woman might arrive, one who looked even more like Rhonda. Or was perhaps Rhonda. So he sat in the café for another two hours. He had forgone breakfast in the Bar Sordello, so he had a croissant, some toast, and several pots of tea. A cannoli accompanied the final pot, a gift of the management. Nobody else arrived who looked remotely like Rhonda. More importantly, Rhonda herself did not make an appearance.

9

Orta San Giulio

Just as ebb always follows flow, there was an inevitability that some event would occur whenever Rhonda and JP were on holiday.

It didn't always directly involve them, like the dog bite incident. But there always seemed to be a notable occurrence that helped the couple remember each particular holiday. William married Kate Middleton when they visited Ferrara. And, when they came to Orta San Giulio four years ago, the Brexit vote took the UK out of Europe. JP recalled feeling alienated by those living in Orta. However, to them, it made little difference if Britain remained in or out of Europe.

After a five-hour train journey, JP fancied a walk into town from Orta Miasino station. The track led downhill anyway, it was shaded, and the sun set slowly across the other side of the lake. The cobbled pathway slopes down from the Sacro Monte di Orta, a complex of chapels and ancient buildings at the top of San Nicolao hill. As the sunlight filtered through the trees along the path, JP began to wind his way down towards the sleepy town of Orta San Giulio. If he narrowed his eyes, he could see the beautiful island that appeared to float just offshore.

There was time for a shower and change of clothes before heading out for a pre-dinner drink. JP sat outside the bar, which stood at the end of the main street. Many people swept past that place, so he left the photo in full view on the table. Some glimpsed at it as they sped upon their way, but nobody approached him about it. Nor did the waiter comment on it either when he returned with a gin and tonic. JP sipped it slowly, enjoying the early evening sunshine.

Dinner had been booked at Locanda dell Orta restaurant before JP left home. The first-floor room was a tiny intimate space with only four tables, making it essential to book. The tables were so close together that everyone in the room could hear each other's conversation. A family of four sat in the farthest corner, looking out of the open doors which led to a Juliet balcony. In the other corner, a young couple shared a romantic evening meal. And adjacent to JP's table was a woman, also eating alone. She lightened their embarrassment with a smile. He nodded and looked over his shoulder to see if the waiter might be coming.

Candles lit the room, and the tables were covered in crisp white tablecloths. The woman waited until JP glanced back in her direction.

"Are you from England? Sorry, I heard you speak to the owner when you arrived."

Her voice was a strange combination of accents. JP prided himself on being able to place someone's origins from their speech. Her voice had West Indian undertones, which he expected because she looked to be of Caribbean descent. But her pronunciation was distinctly Scottish.

JP wanted to nod his response but knew it would be rude to remain silent. And he wanted to learn the root of that accent.

"Yes. Are you from Scotland?"

"I am, yes. I'm from Cumbernauld."

"And where were you from originally?" He expected the name of an island in the West Indies.

The woman read his thoughts. If you can't say something kind, then stay quiet, her mother told her. She could have been cruel and ridiculed the racist undertones of his question. She could have said Falkirk, where she was brought up. But she knew what he meant and so followed her mother's advice.

"My parents came from Montserrat."

"Are you on holiday?"

"No, I moved here last year after my husband died. Our son had already emigrated to Australia."

JP appreciated the use of the word 'our', even though her husband had died. And yet, he still struggled to continue a conversation with a complete stranger. Especially a woman.

"My husband worked as a lorry driver. He died three years ago. It took me a few years, but I finally decided to sell up and move somewhere warmer. I like the Scottish mountains and lochs. Lake Orta captures that, but it has the sunshine too."

Her explanation produced little more than another smile from the adjoining table. She sensed the man's shyness, so she waited for JP to place his order and then spoke.

"People assumed I would return to the Caribbean, even though I have never been there. I was born in Scotland. Not the pretty part but enough to make me Scottish, British, European even."

JP finally realised he would need to contribute something to this conversation. He took comfort in the knowledge that It would only continue until the food arrived.

"Are properties expensive here?"

"Mine is in the town centre and has a beautiful view, and it cost one hundred thousand euros less than I sold my house for."

Good manners on the part of both parties ensured that the conversation fell silent when the food arrived.

Much to the woman's surprise, JP opened the dialogue after the dishes had been cleared from their tables.

"This is a picture of my wife."

The woman took the photograph from him and gazed at it before glancing back at JP.

"And why do you carry the photo with you? Are you a widower too?"

"No," he responded immediately, too sharply in fact, as if the question might be painfully intrusive. "The loss of my wife is only a temporary discomfort. Like a hangover, it hurts but that pain will soon pass." He paused. "The reason for carrying the photograph is two-fold," he explained. "Firstly, because Rhonda has left me and secondly because I'm afraid I might forget what she looks like." Both points were delivered in a whisper.

"How long have you been married?"

"Forty-five years."

"Then how could you forget what she looks like?"

"I forget things lately."

"What do you do for a living?"

"I'm a teacher." He gazed off into the past. "I was a teacher, but I'm retired now."

"I'm not sure you ever stop being a teacher. Did you ever read Mark Twain?"

Did she think he taught literature, he wondered?

"I taught business studies to young adults."

"Did that stop you reading Mark Twain?"

"No, I just didn't get round to it."

"Well, there's still time, Professor. You should try him. He's got plenty of stuff to say, and a lot of it is interesting."

She told him Mark Twain reckoned that the two most important days in our life are the day we are born, and the day we figure out why?

"Yes, always saying clever things was Mark Twain." JP's voice sounded a little cynical. He regretted the tone. After all, the woman was only trying to make civil conversation. He had been embarrassed into joining that conversation and couldn't see a way out.

"Mark Twain had something to say on many things, but he wasn't always right. I'm not sure he appreciated that each person has their own idea of importance in their life. It's not all about me. The day I was born, and the day I realised why," JP explained. But that explanation came out like a surging tide, reminding him less of Mark Twain and more like the ongoing stream of consciousness of James Joyce. The woman ignored the sudden rush of information, and JP regretted giving a stranger his personal advice.

"What was the most significant day in your life Mister?" She paused, waiting for the stranger to tell her his name.

JP hesitated. "Preparé," he replied. "JP to my friends."

"You're French. Sorry, I thought you were English."

"Yes, I suppose much the same way as I thought you were West Indian. I am English, but with a French name." He regretted the unnecessary remark.

The woman reached out her hand, and JP hesitated. Not everyone was prepared to shake a stranger's hand since the pandemic became part of life.

"Ebony," she told him, omitting the surname. She was a black woman of medium build and indeterminable age, though probably past retirement age and might have been much older, but her skin tone and well-managed hair made her look younger. She waited for JP to answer her original question.

"Twain," she reminded him. But he gazed off thoughtfully before coming back to life.

"The first was the day I met my wife," he finally answered. "And the second hasn't happened yet."

The woman smiled at his response but didn't speak herself. She seemed to know he would provide the clarification.

"It will be when I find her again." He returned the photograph to his jacket pocket. "I don't subscribe to Twain's belief that a person's life can be condensed into just two important days. I'm not sure he believed it himself, actually. Anyway, if my life revolves around just two days, what were the other twenty-five thousand for? What is important in life is what you believe to be important."

"And what's that?" she asked without hesitation.

"First and foremost, it is about love. Love of others, not ourselves. Second, it concerns honour, and yet we each have a different perspective of honour. And finally, it is about reparation."

"Reparation for what?"

"I believe each of us knows what we must make amends for."

"And I believe," she replied, "that the *why* that Mark Twain talks about in our lives might be nuttin' at all," she announced with authority and a distinct Caribbean mellowness. "Something we don't even remember. Perhaps it was something we said to someone one day, someone we don't even recall meeting."

JP's thoughts went back to find the person who the old woman might be speaking of. He recalled bumping into Malcolm at the bar in Turin. Malcolm only remembered meeting the famous people in his life and only then at a distance. While he remained lost in his thoughts, the woman continued.

"And maybe the why, wasn't even them, cos they just went off and told someone else. It could be the why in our life is someone we never even met. That's more likely in your job than anyone else, Professor. You telling some student something they think is important. And them telling it to someone else, and that thing changing their life."

JP continued to search his thoughts, hoping to find that moment, but it was lost. He convinced himself he would never find it, just as he might never find Rhonda.

"Maybe that off-the-cuff remark changed the lives of those unknown others," the woman continued. "We don't know. I don't think we're meant to know, or it would all be too overwhelming for us. My people say it's all the work of God, and they may be right. After all, they've been saying it for a couple of thousand years, so it could be there is a God pulling the strings. Even before our God, there were others. The guys who lived here, the Romans, they thought there were lots of Gods all interested in different things."

"Yes," he replied. "Cardea was the Roman Goddess of Door Hinges."

Ebony thought he was joking, but JP rarely joked about such important issues as Roman history.

She laughed, giving JP time to contribute to this one-sided conversation, but he remained lost in his thoughts, worried what Rhonda would think about this situation. The flickering candle continued to bother him. The ambience is too romantic for his sensibility. And, through his thoughts, his new acquaintance just kept on talking.

"I can imagine my God up there laughing at some innocuous comment you might have made to some schoolkid changing the world a hundred years later. Perhaps our why is just a moment in time, so insignificant that we don't even remember it ourselves. That's God joshing with us. No, I think you're right, Mister Preparé, the day you're born has little to do with anything in this world. It's what we do in this world that makes the difference. One tiny word can change everything that is to come."

They ordered their dessert, and the woman invited JP to join her at her table. He hesitated. What would Rhonda think if she walked in at that moment? But he agreed and asked the woman if she wanted a glass of wine. She told him she didn't drink, and he wondered why someone who disliked wine would move to Italy.

JP sipped his wine and dwelt on the woman's extraordinary views on life. Things happen in life, that much was sure. And from those moments, other moments are created. But whatever happens, is meant to happen. No one can make it otherwise. There isn't another world where something different happens, and another future is created. There is only what materialises from our decisions in this world, our successes and failures in this life. Whether that is to turn right instead of left one day, or propose to someone, or do something completely stupid or irrational.

Everything has consequences, but the world doesn't often see those consequences. Just us. We may be the only people who see it because we must live with the world we create.

When JP began hearing the woman's words again, Ebony persisted with her description of the second-floor apartment in Piazza Motta. The Italians call it a terracielo house, she explained.

"Which literally means keep it in the air, or full height house."

JP resurfaced from his meandering thoughts.

"But the word actually refers to any upstairs flat," she continued. "It is tiny. The living area and kitchen are open plan, and there is just one bedroom. But it has a beautiful view of the island sitting in the lake. That view is worth the money I paid for the property."

JP heard the woman's words but was not really listening. He needed to speak. At that moment, he needed to expose his feelings, even if it was to a complete stranger.

"Even now," JP uttered incongruously. "When I'm sitting at home alone, she's still there."

"So why are you looking for her?"

"Love ceases not when a soul its freedom wins." JP couldn't remember where he had heard that phrase. Liza would remember.

"Sometimes, you find stuff when you stop looking for it," Ebony answered. "You ever done that? A year after you were looking for something, you searched the house without finding it. Then, one day, you just stumble on it. It was there all the time. You were just looking in the wrong places. If you stop looking, it doesn't mean you won't find it. Perhaps you need to stop looking, free up your mind. You might just remember where she is."

JP didn't respond. He seemed to be simply giving his thoughts a voice, but now he kept silent. And Ebony felt the need to fill that silence.

"It happened to a friend of mine," she told him.

"Cleopas spent his days like you, looking for someone, an old friend of his. When, all of a sudden, he just bumps into him on the road to Emmaus. There's a painting of that moment in Sienna. And there's another near here, in the Oratory of Novara. I guess Cleopas is meant to be the voice of assurance. Telling us that nothing is really lost."

The woman spoke with all the assuredness of experience, but her knowledge, unlike that of Malcolm, had been garnered from endless hours of reading rather than sitting in front of a TV. JP guessed it was the Bible.

"Now, I'm not suggesting anything you see, but domestic violence is the main cause for women running away. It doesn't have to be actual violence. It can be so subtle the aggressor isn't even aware of it."

"Yes, I know," answered JP with a calmness that surprised him. "Apparently, it's even made its way to Ambridge."

Ebony hadn't heard of Ambridge, so she ignored the comment. "They won't give you any information at a refuge," she replied.

"There was no violence."

"She must have had a reason for leaving, JP."

Her voice lowered an octave. They were sharing a table now, and the conversation quietened. "Normally, it's driven by an inability to face something. Do you have children?"

"Yes."

"Are they about to leave home? You've heard of the empty nest syndrome, I assume."

"They left years ago. Rhonda was glad to see the back of them."

"A big birthday or anniversary coming up?"

"No."

"What was it then?" she asked. "What was there about the future that she felt unable to face? What was on the horizon?"

"Nothing, just the annual holiday."

"Might the holiday represent unhappy memories?"

"No, I don't think so. Although Rhonda would have preferred to go to Bellagio again, rather than Sicily." Maybe it wasn't about unhappy memories, he thought to himself. Perhaps it was about unfulfilled memories.

"What about weddings and funerals?"

"No."

"Were you about to move home?"

"No."

"Moving home is a stressful experience."

"We weren't moving home."

"Was she having an affair?"

"She had an affair, many years ago. I didn't know about it back then. She told me about it a few years ago."

"Why did she feel the need to tell you?"

"It was as if she couldn't keep the secret anymore." He hesitated. "In truth, she probably had too much to drink. It just came out."

"And she told you everything, did she?"

"No, I didn't want to know the details."

"So, you didn't allow her to empty her soul?"

"I suppose not."

"Well, there's the answer in my view. Some men just like to give their wives and family a hard time, although you don't seem like one of those men. They're like Red Admirals, laying their eggs in stinging nettles."

"It wasn't like that."

"Have you checked missing persons? The Police can do stuff, conduct checks."

JP raised a patronising smile. This was the last resort. Rhonda wasn't a missing person. He offered to pay the bill for both of them, but Ebony insisted they shared the cost. When the waiter arrived, he had produced separate bills anyway.

When they parted, outside the restaurant, they shook hands, and he thanked her for keeping him company.

"Old age should be wonderful," JP told her.

"It is wonderful, she insisted. "Look at that tree," she replied, pointing across the street. "A child sees the wonder of it. Then that wonder is lost. And when you become old, you see it again. But it's always there. The wonder is always there, Mister Preparé."

"Que será," he sighed. For JP, life was a tragic lament on the loss of love and memory, told in a monotonous, unvarying voice. His tone contrasted sharply with the lyrical tones of his newly found friend.

"Che sarà", the woman corrected him with a prosaic interpretation of the Italian language.

Orta San Giulio is an ethereal, almost mystical place when the sun falls beyond the horizon. The pastel shades of the day took on a different hue in the hotel bar, and the fusion of rococo and baroque designs drew JP back into the past. He straightened the sharp creases in his trousers and sat down to look out across the lake towards the enchanting island that seemed to float there. He pondered on all the things that might have driven Rhonda away. His rigid morality, inflexible scruples and overly sound moral compass. His mono faceted character and single-mindedness that so easily annoyed people. Rhonda worked so hard not to be one of those people.

Providence with joy and discord portions us happy though numbered days. The thought hovered lightly about his mind but, again, he couldn't remember who wrote or said it. Yet still, the words placated his troubled conscience.

The photo had been shown to several members of the hotel staff. None had recognised Rhonda, even though she had stayed there with JP just four years ago.

One place remained on his tour around Italy, the one that JP had favoured all along. And yet, why would she specifically choose Bellagio? One particular and distinct motive occurred to him, and the gnawing of its rationale made greater sense to his troubled mind. If she left to rekindle the affair, then Bellagio could make absolute sense. Yes, her escape is less about unhappy memories than unfulfilled ones, he convinced himself.

"If you could have only one holiday," Rhonda had asked. "Where would you go? Somewhere different, or somewhere familiar?" JP wasn't sure. "What about you?" he asked. There was no hesitation on Rhonda's part. "Bellagio, of course."

JP and Rhonda first visited the Hotel Belvedere in the summer of 1980. The package holiday included lessons in Italian, which JP attended each day while Rhonda looked after Lester, who was two years old. She befriended a member of the hotel staff. JP remembered her talking about their afternoon chats on the lawn terrace outside their room. Hugo, a young man at that time, still worked at the hotel or, at least, he had been when they visited there last, in 2017. Could Hugo have been the man Rhonda had an affair with? Had she been making love to Hugo while JP attended Italian classes? Had their liaison continued during their later visits to the hotel? JP assured himself otherwise. Rhonda had declared the affair had ended years ago.

JP gazed out across the dark waters of the lake towards the enigmatic island.

Liza, too looked out of a window. It had been a dry summer. Indeed the long dry spell cast ill omens on the oak trees, which shed their leaves like tears, mourning the absence of rain. So deep in the dusk and dark, she thought. It was Browning. Robert, not Elizabeth. She smiled ruefully and jabbed her phone a little more violently than usual.

"Lester, it's Liza."

"Yes, I know."

"I've been talking to Robert."

"Oh good, the relationship is storming ahead then?" He nearly mentioned something about hearing wedding bells but decided against it. Liza ignored the sarcastic comment, anyway.

"He came up with a theory about Dad. He reckons that Dad might be looking for Mum.

"Well, I hope he's got some fairy dust in his pocket."

"This isn't the time for jokes, Lester. We need to do something. Have you had any more thoughts about the password to Dad's computer?"

Much to her surprise, her brother had come up with a suggestion. He recalled their father telling him about his parents' wedding. "Apparently, Dad paid for the wedding from a winning bet on The Derby."

"A bet?" Liza responded incredulously. "Dad never had a bet in his life."

"Or it might have been a sweepstake," Lester confessed. "Anyway, I looked up the winner of the Derby the year they got married, and it was called The Minstrel."

"Hmm! That sounds like a long shot to me," answered Liza.

"No, it wasn't an outsider, but it wasn't the favourite either."

"No, Lester, I mean it's a long shot that Dad had a horse in the sweepstake and that it paid for the wedding."

"Did Mum never mention it to you then?"

"No, she didn't."

"Well, I reckon it could be the password. It is certainly significant because the jockey was Lester Piggott. Don't you see?"

"Right, I'm going over to Dad's house tonight. I'll call you later." She then had an afterthought. "Oh, any news on Girl-A, er Alpha?"

"Like what?"

"Erm, confirmation of parenthood, allocation of gender, Christening party. Anything I can tell Dad when I eventually get to see him."

"I think the word 'undefined' manages to answer all those questions."

JP gazed at the enchanting island, lit up, across the glistening water of the glacial lake. "What about you?" he asked the absent Rhonda. "Bellagio, of course," came the unhesitant response. But she wasn't there. She was somewhere else, in the wrong place, withered by time's decay, something that had gone out of style, like carafes and dessert trolleys.

10

Bellagio

Lost amongst the midmost trees of an unremembered forest, a forfeit paid to time's gnawing hunger. JP stirred from a slumber moulded by the rhythmic clickety-clack of track and wheel. And, emerging into an alien world, he wonders for a moment what he is doing on a train. Then, in that tiny fissure between sleeping and waking, he recalls the third bedroom and his fashioning of a new future from the documents spread upon the bed. He remembers seeking that lost pathway back to past times. Tiny segments of a dream vaporise before him. Love never dies, he reflects. It simply abandons us.

The train arrived in the lakeside city of Como just after lunchtime, and he hoped he had time for a sandwich before boarding the hydrofoil. The final leg of his journey would take less than an hour.

JP wheeled his suitcase to the ferry point to collect a timetable and then returned to the Café Monti across the road to read it. From here, at the most southerly end of the lake, he could see the boats arrive. Some younger travellers taking the same route to the popular resorts in the central region of the lake loitered nearby. Some lay sprawled across their luggage, expecting to be woken by the noisy vessel when it arrived. JP ordered a coffee and removed his glasses. He wiped the lenses before setting them in place. His perfectly formed plan hadn't given much consideration to ferry times. No more ferries were heading north today, and he had just missed the fast hydrofoil that would have taken him to Bellagio before sunset.

The next hydrofoil did not arrive for another two hours. It would reach Bellagio shortly after eight o'clock. He decided to grab something to eat here, in Como. He already felt tired from a long day travelling and, whilst the terrace restaurant at Hotel Belvedere would still be open, he did not want to eat too late.

He finished his coffee and found a little trattoria close to the ferry point, which would serve a dual purpose. It would kill time and provide a plate of fish fresh from the lake. JP remembered visiting the city of Como with Rhonda on a day trip from Bellagio. They went on the funicular railway, up to the town of Brunate, perched high above the city and saw the distant Italian Alps descending into foothills and rushing rivers. The locals called this viewing point the balcony of the Prealps. From this elevated viewing point, one could see for miles along the lake.

He gazed up towards the hilltop town of Brunate. It struck him as strange that he could remember Rhonda sitting on that stone wall, breathless by the high altitude and the incredible view. And yet, he couldn't remember the last time he saw her. JP could also remember sitting on the terrace of Hotel Belvedere in Bellagio enjoying a wonderful meal with his wife. And yet, he could not remember the last meal he ate with her. He remembered the details of that meal three years ago. He could smell the bouquet of the bottle of Ca' Brione they shared, and he could almost taste the piece of cake he had for dessert. So why could he not remember the last meal they enjoyed together at home? It could only have been a few days ago, or perhaps weeks or months? He couldn't even remember that.

Allowing everyone to pass through the gate onto the ramp, JP stowed his well-travelled suitcase among a pile of other luggage and found a seat. To his embarrassment, his phone rang. He loathed having to listen to other people's conversations on public transport. Liza's name flashed on the screen, and he considered simply switching his phone off. But he didn't. His impending departure provided an excellent opportunity to cut the conversation short.

"Hello, Dad. It's Liza."

"Yes, I know. I'm on a hydrofoil, so I can't hear you properly. Can we speak later?"

Liza began to speak just as the engines started up. The noise was deafening.

"I can't hear you," was the last thing she heard before the line went dead.

"It is humane to have compassion for the afflicted," Liza told Lester. She had committed the opening lines of *The Decameron* to her heart and mind when she accompanied her parents to Bellagio for their 25th wedding anniversary, just after her graduation.

The sentiment was most assiduously applied to her father. In honouring her father, such compassion is twice blessed. Yet her diligence, in banishing all pain from his mind and anguish from his heart, only contributed to his disappearing memory. Every good deed shines a light into the darkness, so they say. Yet good deeds rarely go unpunished.

"It is humane to have compassion for the afflicted," Liza repeated as her brother stirred himself.

"Oh, and who is that? Edmund Spenser or some other irrelevant medieval scribbler?"

"It's Boccaccio, actually."

"Well, he's not allowed since Brexit. Stop moaning, will you."

"I'm not a moaner."

"You've always been a moaner. I'm sure Dad still thinks that I gave up the bigger bedroom out of altruism."

"So you keep saying, Lester." She heard him stir at the other end of the line. "I just wanted to make sure you would be around tomorrow."

"You managed to say that as if it was a forgone conclusion that I'd forget."

"Can we skip the usual banter, Lester? I just need to know you will be around tomorrow morning. And I wanted to be confident you would take my call. You must be available. We both need to be there for Dad."

"What's going on, Liza? And what's that noise in the background. It sounds like you're in a railway station or airport."

"I'll explain everything tomorrow. Just don't ignore my call."

"Why can't you tell me now?"

"Because I don't want you speaking to Dad about it before I have the chance to talk with him myself." Liza knew that this particular scenario was unlikely, but she wanted to be sure.

As the sun disappeared behind the distant hills across the lake, JP disembarked, heavily legged from the hydrofoil. The night air cools slowly on the long summer days around Lake Como. It departs with the shortening shadows, which evolve and fade like charcoal frescoes along the stony lakeside pathways. The water is crystal clear, but there have been fewer fish in the lake since they first came here. There would be no need to show the photo. He would just need to ask the staff as they were familiar with Rhonda from their previous visits.

Bellagio was the last holiday they had together before the Covid-19 pandemic of 2020. Rhonda and JP spent a long weekend at the Hotel Belvedere in the late summer of 2019 before the world was changed by a tiny pathogen. Their trip to Antibes had been a little disappointing. For JP, France could never replace Italy, and Rhonda couldn't help imagining how smug her late father-in-law would have been, seeing them holidaying in his beloved France. In truth, they both preferred lakes to the sea, even the Mediterranean Sea.

Moreover, they missed the familiarity of the people in Bellagio and, in particular, the special connection they felt for the Hotel Belvedere, probably because they had spent several special anniversaries there. So, following the Antibes holiday, they agreed to take a second break, a few days in Bellagio.

Rhonda said she wished they could condense all their holidays into one fabulous summer. But JP wasn't sure if he had dreamt that conversation.

JP didn't relish the idea of pulling a suitcase up the dauntingly high steps leading to the upper part of the town. So he took the longer, winding road that swept up past the Grand Villa Serbelloni Hotel. He could have telephoned the Hotel Belvedere to request that someone collect him from the ferry point. But he loathed asking for special treatment. Anyway, he'd walked this slow incline many times with Rhonda after returning from days out on the ferries.

As he passed the small infant school at the edge of town, he couldn't help wondering how none of this would have happened if he hadn't decided to change schools at sixth form. If he had continued his education at his secondary school, he would not have met Rhonda. They would never have gone to university together. And they wouldn't have got married. Lester wouldn't exist, nor would Liza. Somewhere, he thought, a parallel universe exists, a sombre place where they never met. As he approached the top of the hill, he felt isolated in that desolate place.

As he approached the hotel and the steep ascent began to level out, he recognised a young man walking towards him. It was Hugo, and he considered asking him if he had seen Rhonda. But he chose not to. He would soon find out if he had been right all along.

"Hello, Hugo."

"Buona sera, Mister Preparé", the stocky sixty-year-old answered. JP felt unsure of his feelings. Pleased that the man remembered him but equally perturbed that he had. "Welcome back," he added.

"You've been here a long time, haven't you, Hugo."

Hugo nodded and went to move off, back to his work about the grounds of the hotel.

"You were here when we first visited the hotel more than forty years ago, weren't you?"

"Trainee gardener," he answered with a smile.

"You must like it here."

"Yes, I am Head Gardener now."

JP wanted to ask so much more but smiled and walked through the open double doors into the hotel reception area. Reaching into his inside jacket pocket to retrieve his passport, JP was distracted as he approached the counter. With his free hand, he attempted to lean the suitcase against a decorative pillar. At the same time, he glanced off into the adjacent lounge area, to where Rhonda used to sit each morning to catch up with the news from home. The case fell to the ground with a loud bang, and JP caught his breath. It was her. It was Rhonda, sitting in the lounge, reading a copy of *The Times*. She looked just as she did on their twenty-fifth wedding anniversary. Her hair looked different, and he could only see part of her face above the newspaper. But it was her. As he opened his mouth to speak, the woman raised her eyes and lowered the newspaper.

"Oh, hello, Dad. Sorry did I surprise you?"

"Liza, what are you doing here?"

JP turned a little pale and seemed breathless. She stood up and looked at her exhausted father. Worries about his welfare surfaced as she looked into his tired eyes. Liza had chosen not to meet him at the ferry point for this very reason. And, for the same reason, Liza decided not to speak with him about her mother until the morning.

JP slumped into one of the armchairs.

"Are you okay, Dad? Do you want a drink of water?"

The Manageress, Laura, appeared next to them as if by magic, holding a glass of water. JP took a sip, and she took the passport from his hand.

"I'll check you in, Mr Preparé. You sit here with your daughter for a moment."

"Are you staying here, Liza?" JP asked his daughter.

"Yes, but I was waiting for you to arrive to check how long you were planning to stay."

"Mr Preparé is booked in for two nights," answered Laura.

"Then I'll stay for two nights if you have a room available."

"Actually, the room next to your father's is free, Miss Prepare."

"Er, I'm sure my daughter would prefer a room by the pool," JP interjected.

Liza smiled. He was showing signs of recovery already.

"Is something wrong?" JP asked a little nervously.

"No, I was just concerned about you travelling around Europe on your own. Although I believe I now know what is going on."

"Going on? Nothing is going on, Liza. I'm simply looking for your mum."

"Yes, Robert said it might be that."

Laura returned to the lounge with JP's passport.

"Your luggage has been taken to your room, Mr Preparé. It's room 502." She handed him the room key and held another towards Liza. "We have room 510 available with a lake view. It's below the restaurant. Would you like me to show you to the rooms?"

"That won't be necessary," JP answered. Liza smiled and took the key.

"You look exhausted, Dad. Where have you travelled from today?"

"Orta," he answered, but the reply didn't sound convincing.

"Have you eaten?"

"Yes, I had to wait for the hydrofoil, so I had lunch in Como."

"You need an early night, Dad. Let's meet for breakfast, shall we?"

She looked into his eyes and saw a lost soul.

He nodded his head, and she sighed in relief. She would tell him tomorrow. The truth would be revealed then, not now at the end of a weary day. Not just before he retired to a strange, darkened bedroom and then left to dwell on his pain. No, the truth would be unwrapped in the sunshine of an Italian summer and the company of a caring daughter.

When they had unpacked, and her father had retired to bed, Liza returned to the lounge for a nightcap. She realised now how she had contributed to the problem.

Being a dutiful daughter, and in her mother's absence, Liza cleaned the house for her father. Her mother's clothing, jewellery and passport had been packed into a suitcase. Out of sight and out of mind, she thought to herself. She also took her mother's mobile phone.

When Liza realised that her father was calling it every day, she kept it charged up. He clearly wanted to listen to the message Rhonda had left, even though it said no more than 'hi, this is Rhonda.' He had heard the recording in Juan le Pins, and again when he checked into the Hotel Annunziata at Ferrara. 'Please leave a message, and I'll call you back.' He listened to the promise many times. And, each time he called her, he waited patiently, not just to hear her voice, but in the hope that she would finally pick the call up. She never did, and he never left a message. What he had to say was not to be left on a voicemail but delivered in person.

Liza went back to her room and called her brother. She confessed her part in confusing their father and explained how Robert had guessed what had happened.

"We'll be home in a couple of days. We just need to keep a close eye on Dad for a while." Tomorrow, she thought things past and things imagined would rise from their slumber.

And so it was. The following morning, a blighted past and a fragile future sat down together. JP listened patiently to his daughter's explanation, doubting at first, then gazing, heavy-hearted and torn by her words. But, as he was lifted from the void by the realisation of truth, there was no sense of liberation, only misery and wretched embarrassment to accompany it.

Liza watched as the truth tore her father apart. The pretence that Rhonda was alive and just ahead of him on the road had been unveiled as no more than a mirage that slowly evaporated before his eyes. It wasn't some childish attempt to hide from the truth. The truth had been kept from him by the body's urge to survive. He knew she had gone but hadn't noticed where or when. And after the pain, there came unremitting shame that he could forget such a thing, that he could mislay such a memory and forget Rhonda had died.

Liza needed to take her father back, relive those sad events, and inflict unimagined pain.

As Spring turned to Summer and the bluebells died beneath the oaks, Rhonda caught Covid-19. Visitors were not allowed during her short stay in the hospital. JP didn't see her for her last days on earth, and Liza took care of the funeral arrangements. It was a small affair for family members only.

Robert worked out what happened next and tried to explain it to Liza. Her father could not accept the truth, so he fashioned a new past to his own design. JP created a world where Rhonda still lived. And, once he did this, there followed a need to reinforce that new vision with evidence. His wife had an affair, or so he believed. He used this as corroboration to substantiate and establish a reason for her disappearance. It was understandable. Rhonda had fallen ill one day and was admitted to hospital with Covid-19. Restrictions in place during the pandemic meant JP could not visit her. He did not witness her passing from this world. He saw no evidence of her death. So, it was easy to imagine it had not happened. JP was a planner, a person with the ability to create a future from his own imagination. Planning the ideal life had been no more difficult for him than arranging the perfect holiday or even condensing all their holidays into one fabulous summer, as Rhonda had suggested. Creating a future to one's own design is simple. So why not the past and the present too?

Yes, Robert guessed what happened in those lost days after Rhonda died. He couldn't pinpoint the actual moment, but he could understand why JP ran off to search for Rhonda around Europe. In reality, JP could not accept his wife's death and, as a coping mechanism, he convinced himself she had run away. His search for her in Italy proved fruitless, yet it had been a poignant and cathartic experience. It represented no more than a psychological defence that anyone might use to reduce anxiety when something feels particularly disturbing.

"Perhaps not quite as extreme as this," explained Robert, "because he does seem to believe the narrative completely."

"Why didn't I notice it happening?" asked Liza.

"There was no pivotal moment. It's not a concussion. Your father just went to sleep one night in the knowledge that your mother had died, and then he woke up in the morning convinced she had just left home."

Liza feared she may have been responsible for passing Covid-19 on to her mum. After all, she had taken the voluntary position at the hospital and could easily have caught it there. But nothing was ever mentioned of this, for it would simply cause further anguish to her already distraught father.

After breakfast, Liza and JP went for a walk in the Melzi Gardens that runs along the lakeside. The Rhododendron and Azalea that bordered the meandering pathways through the private estate had lost their colourful flowers. And, as the pair strolled along, JP told Liza what he knew of Rhonda's affair, which was very little.

"She allowed a man to take advantage of her. She felt ashamed. I didn't want to know the details," he confessed. "To be honest, I think I've worked out who it was and when it happened, Liza."

Liza went to speak but was prevented by her father. "No, this is important, very important, because it has consequences. I believe your mother had an affair with the gardener at the hotel back in 1980."

"Hugo?"

"Yes."

"But, Dad."

"No, let me finish," he insisted. "You will be able to work this out for yourself, but you were born the following year." He hesitated, caught his breath and gazed out across the lake. Liza seized the moment.

"Dad, will you please stop. Firstly, Mum did not have an affair. And, secondly, Hugo is gay."

"Really? Gay? Are you sure? Anyway, how can you possibly know that your mum didn't have an affair? It happened before you were born."

"Because I thought about what you said. And I wondered why Mum hadn't told me about this so-called affair. Then I realised that she *had* told me. I just didn't jump to the same assumption as you did that she had an affair."

"What was it then, if it wasn't an affair?"

"Dad, the incident you are thinking about was something entirely different. She didn't say she had an affair. She said that she had let you down. Mum had already told me about the incident, and it was so trivial I'd forgotten about it. It was when she invested the money her parents left her in a Ponzi scheme during the Big Bang of 1980. She lost all her inheritance. She was distraught, and it took her ages to bring herself to tell you. And, when she did, you didn't want to know. She assumed you thought it was her money, and she could do what she liked with it."

"I'd never thought about her inheritance." He sighed inwardly at his own stupidity. "So, she didn't have an affair?"

"No, Dad, she didn't."

"And Hugo is gay, is he?"

"Yes, I spoke with him this morning, actually. He and Mum became good friends during your first visit here and used to chat every morning. He's a fascinating character. Unlike the UK, homosexuality has been legal in Italy since the nineteenth century, although not considered acceptable behaviour, of course. Well, certainly not to Italian mothers. The seventies was a revolutionary period in Milan, but it did not extend to the suburbs. So he ran away when he was sixteen and joined a commune in a fifteenth-century palazzo near the Duomo in the city. But that didn't work out, and he came here a short time later. He has worked as a gardener at the hotel ever since."

JP shook his head in the realisation of how stupid he had been. "I'm not surprised he liked your mother. She is... was much more tolerant than me, even in those dark days of the seventies and eighties. I'm still not sure how I would react if you or Lester were." JP hesitated, unable to speak the word.

"Well, you won't need to face that particular situation, Dad. It seems that you may be a grandfather."

"What do you mean, might be?"

"Well, there's this girl called Tabatha, who's a keen supporter of the transgender movement. She's had a baby, and it might be Lester's. But she doesn't believe in children being possessions. Babies are self-identifying entities, apparently. Oh, and it's a girl to you or me, but to Tabatha, the baby is neither. She's an *it*."

"Slow down, Liza. Girlfriend, baby girl."

His daughter's confusing statement seemed like a bucket of ice water over JP's already disoriented thoughts. Hugo is gay, Rhonda did not have an affair, and now he is or might be a grandfather. Those thoughts rushed like a tsunami through his mind.

"What do they call *it* then?"

"Girl-A."

"Isn't that a little bit of a giveaway?"

"That's what I said, Dad. Anyway, she answers to Alpha too."

"Alpha?"

"It's all supposed to be ironic. Pathetic might be a better word," Liza sighed.

"Lester's always done his own thing."

"He's always taken you for a ride, Dad."

"Our fault for naming him after a jockey, I suppose."

Liza was pleased to see he was getting his sense of humour back.

"Will I get to see her, er it?" he asked. "What do I call it? Not granddaughter, obviously. Grandnonbinary doesn't really work, does it?"

"Never mind now, Dad. They'll come around. The world imposes its own will on everyone eventually – even Lester."

"Your mum and I used to walk through these gardens every time we visited Bellagio. There's a lovely restaurant at the other end."

"Yes, I know, we lunched there on your fortieth anniversary."

"Yes, of course," he muttered as he remembered that day. "How could I forget?" He now realised just how much he had forgotten. "And there's a statue of

Dante and Beatrice by the folly, halfway through the garden."

"Yes, I remember it."

It amazed him that she still remembered such detail of their holiday together.

"How could I have forgotten?" JP murmured.

Liza knew instinctively that her father was referring to her mother's death and not the lunch in Loppia.

"We didn't even say goodbye. We had known each other for more than forty years. I don't remember saying hello to her at the beginning, nor do I recall saying goodbye at the end. How can that be after all these years?"

"It was Covid, Dad. Nobody got to say goodbye."

JP felt his chest tighten a little. He didn't want to cry in front of Lisa. There would be plenty of time for tears later. He held his eyes open and, as they walked towards the small town of Loppia, he changed the subject, knowing any topic from the past would lead back to Rhonda.

"Do you remember Lucky?"

"Our cat? Blackie? Yes, of course. You told us he'd gone back to his mummy. Which he had in a way, I suppose."

JP looked at her with a guilty expression.

"Don't worry, Dad. The kids at number ten told us the cat had been run over," Liza confessed. "Lester and I didn't mention it to you because you seemed quite shook up by it."

Liza waited for her father to finish his story. The gap grew, and she wondered if he'd forgotten the point he was trying to make. He had lost the thread of a conversation a few times recently.

JP then sighed. "Your mum said that death should be embraced as part of life, not the end of it." He smiled at his daughter. "As usual, she was right."

The old woman of Orta was right too, and JP required little persuasion towards her beliefs. The future is the most fragile of creatures and may be diverted by the least significant of events. Life needs no other devices than its own capriciousness. The gods mock us, JP convinced himself. Particularly those like him and Henri Fayol, who attempt to outwit chance with planning.

When the sun rose on their last day in Bellagio, JP recalled the moment he forgot his wife had died. A week after her funeral, he decided to return to Italian language classes. But halfway there, he stopped, changed his mind and returned home. It seemed pointless learning Italian if there was never to be holidays again. He fumbled with the key and stumbled inside the hallway. He couldn't make it any further. He fell to his knees, and the full realisation of his loss overpowered him. He curled up on the floor, unable to move, sobbing until eventually, he fell asleep there in the hallway. A few hours later, he stirred, cold and bemused, wondering where he was. Half asleep, he undressed and fell on the bed. For the love of Rhonda, he vowed never to wake.

By God's grace, his anguish lasted that night only, for he slept in the shadow of compassion. In the morning, he remembered nothing of his wife's passing. He believed Rhonda had gone away. Any memory of her illness, death and funeral were lost.

Through Liza's kind words, he had woken forever from that dream. After breakfast, the pair packed their suitcases and walked down to Pescallo, a small village sitting on the lakeside at the foot of the hill below the hotel. Rhonda walked there most mornings when they stayed at the Belvedere. She liked feeding the ducks that swam about the still arm of the lake that ran down to Lecco.

"I managed to get a seat on the same flight as you, Dad."

"Good, the company will be nice."

Liza took his arm and made him walk on a little quicker. She pulled a bread roll from her pocket.

"For the ducks," she declared.

"I'm not sure I can do this again," JP told her.

"What? Feed the ducks?"

"No, travel around Europe. It isn't the same without your Mum. I'm not built to make memories alone. Anyway, I'd sooner have the ones I've already made with your mum."

"You might not need a holiday in the future," she told him. "Robert is overseeing some work in your garden. It's our treat. Robert fancies himself as a garden designer, so you will notice some changes when you get home. He's creating a slice of Italy in your back garden."

"That's very kind of you."

"It's only Robert indulging himself, Dad. There will be a lovely wide set of stone steps between the oak trees and some large terracotta pots filled with basil plants. Your own little piece of Italy."

"I love basil. The smell reminds me of Italian summers," JP smiled. "I'll be able to sit in my garden and imagine I'm in Italy." He squeezed her hand. "I shall just lounge around and gaze up, thinking of past holidays with your mum, remembering the blue above the trees."

The Blue above the Trees

The Blue above the Trees takes inspiration from *Isabella, or the Pot of Basil*, a poem by John Keats that is itself inspired by a tale from Boccaccio's *The Decameron*. Each of the narratives tells a poignant story of lost love. All things to end are made. Life and plague alike, fondness and fear, admiration and desperation. And the last of these to pass shall be love. As in Keats's *Isabella, or the Pot of Basil*, there follows a voyage of discovery.

> *When the full morning came, she had devised*
> *how she might secret to the forest hie;*
> *how she might find the clay, so dearly prized,*
> *and sing to it one latest lullaby;*

Keats found inspiration for his poem *Isabella, or the Pot of Basil*, in Boccaccio's *The Decameron*.

> *Once she got up that morning, having no wish to say anything to her brothers, she determined to go to the place he had shown her and to see if what she had seen in her dream were true.*

And *The Blue above the Trees* takes inspiration from both Boccaccio and Keats.

> *The sprawling Bougainvillea*
> *and intoxicating aroma of Basil*
> *now summon him from a distant land,*
> *where she may be found shrouded midst that fragrance.*

Printed in Great Britain
by Amazon